# CASSIDY

## Wayne D. Overholser

Chivers    •    Thorndike Press
Bath, England     Waterville, Maine USA

This Large Print edition is published by BBC Audiobooks Ltd, England, and by Thorndike Press, USA.

Published in 2003 in the U.K. by arrangement with the author c/o Golden West Literary Agency.

Published in 2003 in the U.S. by arrangement with Golden West Literary Agency.

U.K. Hardcover   ISBN 0–7540–7267–3  (Chivers Large Print)
U.K. Softcover    ISBN 0–7540–7268–1  (Camden Large Print)
U.S. Softcover    ISBN 0–7862–5412–2  (Nightingale Series)

The text of this Large Print edition is unabridged.
Other aspects of the book may vary from the original edition.

Set in 16 pt. New Times Roman.

Printed in Great Britain on acid-free paper.

---

**British Library Cataloguing in Publication Data available**

---

**Library of Congress Cataloging-in-Publication Data**

Overholser, Wayne D., 1906–
      Cassidy / Wayne D. Overholser.
         p.    cm.
     ISBN 0–7862–5412–2 (lg. print : sc : alk. paper)
     1. Wyoming—Fiction. 2. Fathers—Death—Fiction.
     3. Revenge—Fiction. 4. Large type books. I. Title.
     PS3529.V33C36 2003
     813'.54—dc21                  2003047782

# CHAPTER ONE

My name is Bruce Cassidy. It's my real name and I'm proud of it. In most ways I'm a rational man, but there is one exception. Ever since I was ten years old I have hated big cowmen.

I am very much aware that this is not a rational feeling. It's the kind I can't do anything about, that goes right into the bottom of my belly and makes me want to strike out at any of them whenever I have a chance. There's a reason for my feeling that way and I'll tell you about it presently.

I was riding for Marge Delaney when the opportunity of a lifetime came along. At least that was the way it seemed to me. Marge was an old maid in her forties, twice my age, so there was nothing romantic between us. She was tall and thin and as tough as whang leather, but I liked and respected her.

Marge owned the K Bar. It was in the foothills of the Blue Mountains out of Baker City a piece, not a big spread, just big enough to give Marge a living if she was let alone, but she was surrounded by Horsehead range and Horsehead was owned by Jason Quinlan. Quinlan was a big cowman and a range hog, a perfect example of the kind I hated, and I guess that was the reason I'd gone to work for

Marge and had stayed on, even though she was always behind in my pay.

I rode in late one spring afternoon, having spent the day looking over the Battle Creek range to see if it was time to move our cattle. They'd eaten up just about everything on our valley range and we weren't sure whether the grass was up enough along Battle Creek to warrant moving our stock. The altitude was a good deal higher than our lower range, so it was always well into the spring or early summer before we could drive our cattle onto it.

Marge must have seen me coming. She ran out of the house when I was still fifty yards away. Two other cowboys worked for her, but they were old and bunged up with rheumatism so neither could do a day's work. Put together they made a pretty good man, but I was the one she leaned on. Everybody knew it, so there was never any hard feelings when I took over, even though I was only twenty-one.

As soon as I stopped, I said, 'The grass ain't up yet. Not enough. We'll have to let 'em root around down here for another week yet, maybe more.'

I figured that was why she'd come out to the corral to meet me, but right away I saw it wasn't. She'd been crying, and that was the last thing you'd expect Marge to do. In fact, in the year I'd been working for her, I'd never known her to come close to crying.

2

She didn't say anything. I guess she couldn't right then. The corners of her mouth were working and her chin was trembling, so I knew all hell must have busted loose. I stepped down and moved up close to her, staring at her because this was a new Marge and I didn't know what to make of her.

'What happened?' I asked.

'They were out here this afternoon,' she said.

'They?'

'Quinlan,' she said. 'And the Harrigan twins.'

I wasn't surprised. They'd never been here before, but Quinlan wanted the K Bar and he'd put all the pressure he could on Marge to sell to him and stay inside the law. Before I'd started working for the K Bar, Quinlan had run off, scared off, or killed off all the small ranchers who had been Marge's neighbors.

She was the only one left, the K Bar now an island in a Horsehead sea, and that was a tribute to Marge's toughness. It had helped to be a woman, but the fact remained that she had to be tough or she wouldn't still be here, woman or not.

'What did Quinlan want?' I asked.

'The K Bar,' she said bitterly. 'He's given us twenty-four hours to sell out to him and move. If we're not gone by three o'clock tomorrow afternoon, they're coming in to burn us out and they'll kill us if we make a stand.'

3

'I thought we'd gone past that kind of shenanigan,' I said. 'Looks like the law doesn't mean as much to him as he's been letting on.'

'I told him I'd go to the sheriff and he laughed in my face,' she said. 'The sheriff's gone fishing and he'll be gone for a week. By the time he gets back, it'll be all over. You know the sheriff won't move against Quinlan once something's already happened.'

That was true. I guess I'd known all along that sooner or later Quinlan would make a move like this. He hadn't paid any attention to the law in the past. There was no reason to think he would now.

I'd never told myself in plain words, but I knew the only reason I'd gone to work for Marge in the first place was to get a whack at Quinlan. Not that I had anything against him personally. He was a big cowman. That was reason enough to hate him.

'He's never buffaloed you before,' I said.

'He's never come right out and done this before,' she said. 'I can do a day's work when he scares off my hands and I can grow a garden and butcher a beef so we'll have something to eat when the store cuts off my credit, but I can't let you and Mike and Chuck get killed trying to hold off Quinlan's tough hands.'

This was another side of her I'd never seen before. I had figured that when the showdown came, she'd be all for burning some powder,

4

but no, she was worrying about me and two broken down old cowpokes who weren't worth their salt. I had no idea how much Quinlan had said, but he sure had put the fear of the Lord into Marge Delaney.

'Where is he now?' I asked. 'Did he go back to Horsehead?'

'No,' she answered. 'He said he'd stay in town tonight and he'd be in the hotel if I decided to sell before three. If I didn't, I'd see him and his men out here.'

I turned and stepped into the saddle. She cried, 'Bruce, where are you going?'

'To town,' I said. 'Where'd you think I was going?'

'What are you fixing to do?'

'I'm going to clean Quinlan's plow for him,' I said. 'What else is there to do?'

'No, Bruce. You're not going to do no such thing. I'll sell to him. I'm getting tired trying to make a little spread go and he's made a fair offer. I'll let him have it and move into Baker City. You don't need to worry. He'll give you a job. He promised.'

That made me laugh. Going to work for a big outfit like Horsehead was the last thing I wanted to do. I said, 'Marge, you always were a hell of a poor liar. I'll see you after while.'

'Wait, Bruce.' She grabbed my leg with both hands and stood looking up at me. 'Now you listen. I don't want any trouble. I know I've talked tough in the past, but now that it's here,

5

I can't face it. I told you he had the Harrigan twins with him. He always does. You might outdraw one of them, but you can't whip both of them.'

I'd heard plenty about the Harrigan twins since I'd started working for the K Bar. They were about thirty and I doubt that either of them had ever done a day's work in his life. They were gunslicks, the kind you read about and never think you'll see. They both wore two guns, and that was something else you don't expect to see. They were always with Quinlan, so they were actually his bodyguards.

I'd never seen the Harrigans in action, but I'd heard enough about their gun fights to accept the fact that they were mean and ornery and damned fast on the draw. But then I'd faced some fast men and I was still kicking and they weren't, so I was brash enough to figure I could handle them.

'I figure I can do the job, Marge,' I said. 'When I get done with them, I'll change Quinlan's mind.'

'You get off that horse right now, Bruce Cassidy,' she shouted. 'I don't know why I told you about it. I don't even know why I didn't sell out to Quinlan a long time ago. Nobody's ever kept anything from him that he's wanted, and I don't know why I thought I could.'

'I'll tell you why, Marge,' I said. 'It's because your pa pioneered this country. He started the K Bar and you grew up on it in the days before

6

Quinlan showed up, when people could live where they pleased. I'll tell you one more thing. You told me about this business because you knew I could do something about it. Now let go of my leg and I'll go do it.'

Her face turned red and I knew that she knew that what I'd said was the truth. She let go and stepped back, then she said in a hard tone, 'If you ride into town and kick up a fuss with the Harrigans, you're fired.'

'All right, Marge,' I said. 'Just have my pay ready when I come back for my gear.'

I rode toward town and didn't look back, but I'm damned if I didn't hear her crying. I didn't figure on that, either. She had a soft side to her I'd never known was there. I guess she liked me. We'd always got along, though she had a prickly disposition that made me think she didn't really like anybody. I guess you just never know about people, particularly women.

## CHAPTER TWO

Baker City was the county seat and the biggest town in Baker County, but it was twenty miles away and we seldom went there unless we had business with the county officials or it was shipping time. To us Delaney meant town. It was named after Marge's pa and was only two miles from the K Bar.

Delaney wasn't much of a town and probably never would be because there weren't many people living in our end of the county. Actually there were less now than there had been several years ago. The decrease was due to Horsehead gobbling up the small outfits. I wasn't here when Quinlan was roughing up Marge's neighbors, but from what I heard, he must have driven at least ten families out of the country.

I rode into town a little after six and tied in front of the hotel. Besides the hotel, there were two saloons, one store, one blacksmith shop, one livery stable, and maybe a dozen dwellings on boths ends of the business block, most of them log cabins.

The hotel had a bar, a lobby, and a dining room, and was the social center of town. The important men like Quinlan always did their drinking in the hotel bar, leaving the saloons for the cowboys and anyone else who wasn't on top of the social pile.

I figured Quinlan would be eating supper this time of day, but I was lucky. He was sitting in the lobby smoking a cigar and whittling on a stick of wood, white shavings on the floor all around his chair. One thing was sure. He wouldn't be sweeping up the mess he'd made.

No one else was in the lobby except the clerk behind the desk. I hadn't decided how I'd play my hand because everything depended on where the Harrigans were. I guessed they were in the bar. I paused just a moment inside the door as I took a quick look at the lobby.

The clerk said, 'Howdy, Bruce.'

I nodded and said, 'Howdy, Joe.'

Quinlan looked up, saw who I was, and went on whittling, his lips curling down around his cigar in a mean expression. I guess he knew why I was there and maybe he wished the Harrigans were with him. I had a fair reputation in the southern part of the state as a gun-hand, but I'd never been in a gunfight in Baker County and I doubt that my reputation had crossed the Blue Mountains, so maybe Quinlan didn't give me a second thought.

Jason Quinlan was a mean son of a bitch. It takes a certain kind of arrogant, grasping, brutal, domineering bastard to be a big cowman. I could think of a few more descriptive words, but those will do. To be rational about it, which I knew I wasn't, I have to admit that some big cowmen are decent human beings, but Quinlan didn't belong to that category.

He was a big man, six feet two or three, about fifty, and he'd weigh maybe 250 pounds, running more to fat than to muscle. He didn't have any neck, or none that I could see. He had a bulldog jaw and thick lips, and he had a way of looking over or around or below any man he didn't figure was his equal. To him I was just a K Bar cowhand.

Quinlan sat with his chair canted back

against the wall. It took me about ten deliberate steps to cross to him. I didn't say a word. I hooked my right foot under the bottom rung of his chair and I yanked it out from under him.

He let out a squall like a stepped-on pup and he hit the floor with a crash you could have heard in the street. I wheeled and walked into the bar, knowing he might shoot me in the back, but hoping he was too shaken up to even think of it. Besides, I had a notion his pride was bruised more than his hind end.

I expected to meet the Harrigans running from the bar into the lobby to see what the racket was, but I didn't, so they must have been in the dining room. No one was in the bar except the bartender and a little, dried up gent who had the most leathery, deep-lined face I ever saw in my life.

I didn't stop to discuss the time of day with either the little gent or the barkeep, but went right on to the far end of the room, then turned and faced the street door. The bartender came toward me, asking, 'What'll it be, Bruce?'

'Nothing,' I said. 'What I came in for will be showing up from the lobby in about half a minute.'

He took a look at my face and didn't say a word, but moved back along the bar. I was right. I don't think it was half a minute until one of the Harrigans came through the lobby

10

door. He took two steps into the bar, then spotted me and stopped. I didn't know which one he was and it didn't make any difference. Mostly I was wondering where his brother was.

The bartender moved back toward me. The Harrigans were just as arrogant and domineering as their boss and most folks in town hated them as much as I did. I didn't know why the bartender had moved back toward me until I heard him say, soft-like, 'The street door, Bruce.'

The Harrigan who had come in from the lobby stood there motionless for maybe twenty seconds, pinning his gaze on me so I'd feel dead before he made his draw. His eyes were pale blue and held no more expression than if they were made of glass. It did give me a prickly feeling along my spine to look at the bastard.

'You know what you just done, Cassidy?' Harrigan asked. 'When you yanked that chair out from under Mr. Quinlan, you committed suicide. I'm going to fill you so full of holes they won't find enough of you to bury.'

The second Harrigan stood in the street doorway. He didn't move and he didn't say a word. If the bartender hadn't said anything, I might not even have noticed the gunman. That, of course, was the game. The first one who had come in from the lobby would talk and get my attention, then he'd tell me to make my play, but before he got the words

11

said, the one in front would have his gun out of leather, so I didn't hesitate. I went for my gun.

I never had been one to wait when I knew I was going to kill a man, and it was a good thing I didn't. The Harrigan standing by the lobby door was talking again, but I don't know what he said. The other one had already started his draw.

I beat him by just enough to keep me alive and to kill him. I got him right through the brisket, then I dived to the floor and rolled, something I'd learned to do a long time ago and had practised by the hour when I was younger.

The Harrigan standing beside the lobby door let go just as I went down. He got in two fast shots, both bullets ripping into the bar where I'd been standing. By that time I was on my belly tipping my gun and pulling the trigger. My first shot caught Harrigan in the guts, the second one in the throat as he went down.

It was over that quick. I got up, reloaded, and looked at the bartender. I said, 'I reckon you saw how it was in case the sheriff wants to know.'

'I sure did, Bruce,' he said, pop-eyed. 'I never seen better shooting in my life. You had no choice. They came in here to kill you.'

I stepped over the Harrigan who lay near the lobby door and dropped my gun back into the holster as I went into the lobby. Quinlan was sitting in his chair, but this time it wasn't canted back against the wall. He didn't expect to see me, and the instant he saw who it was, his face turned a bilious greenish-white.

'The Harrigans' luck ran out, Quinlan,' I said. 'You sent them in there to kill me, but now they're dead and I'm alive. You're wearing a gun. Get up and try doing the job yourself.'

He still couldn't say a word and he couldn't move. The clerk called in a scared voice, 'Cassidy, don't do it.'

I eased over to the desk. Without taking my eyes off Quinlan, I said to the clerk, 'Joe, this bastard rode out to the K Bar with the Harrigans this afternoon and ordered Marge to sell or they'd burn her out by tomorrow at three. Now what kind of man would do that to a woman?'

Quinlan licked his lips, eyes bulging as if they were about to pop out of their sockets. The clerk said, 'The hell he did! I thought Horsehead had all the range he needed.'

'He has,' I said. 'Did you ever know a range hog to quit trying to get more?'

'No,' the clerk said, still scared. 'I never did.'

'I wasn't there when he showed up at the K Bar with the Harrigans,' I said, 'but I'm here now. I'm listening, Quinlan. What have you got to say?'

I stood looking at him, my right hand on my gun butt. He opened his mouth and licked his

13

lips and shut his mouth, and not a word came out. I said, 'Look at him, Joe. He ain't promised to let Marge alone. I reckon I ought to shoot him. That's the only way she'll be safe.'

'Not in here,' Joe yelled. 'Get him outside.'

'He can't talk,' I said. 'Looks like he can't move, either.'

'I won't make no more trouble for her,' Quinlan said in a squeaky voice.

'Well now,' I said. 'Joe, did you hear that? He made a promise.'

'I heard,' the clerk said.

I walked toward Quinlan, not stopping until I was about five feet from him. 'If you break that promise, Quinlan, I'll kill you. It doesn't make any difference how far away I am, I'll hear about it and I'll come back and kill you. Do you savvy that?'

'I savvy,' he said.

I stood there another ten seconds just staring at him, but he wasn't staring back. His gaze was on the floor. He was only half a man, the most hang-dog looking critter I ever saw in my life.

I turned and strode out of the lobby. I untied my horse, thinking I'd get my pay from Marge, pick up my gear, and start riding. I wasn't sure where I'd go, but there wasn't any sense staying on here. Marge would be sorry she'd fired me and she'd beg me to stay, but I'd been here long enough. Somewhere, maybe

14

in Wyoming or Montana, I'd find another chance to whittle down a big cowman.

I had raised my foot to the stirrup when the little gent who'd been at the bar came charging out through the batwings, hollering, 'Mr. Cassidy. Just a minute, Mr. Cassidy.'

I put my foot back on the ground and turned. 'I've got no business with you,' I said. 'I'm riding.'

'You might have some business with me if you'd listen,' he said. 'I'm offering you a job. One hundred dollars when you agree to take it and one hundred dollars every month that you're on the job.'

'Where?'

'Wyoming.'

I tied my horse again. I said, 'We'll talk about it.'

## CHAPTER THREE

The little gent's name was Chauncey Dunn. We went up to his room and he got out a whisky bottle and offered me a drink. I said I didn't use it. That seemed to please him.

'A man who's as good with his gun as you are shouldn't drink,' he said. 'I've seen some good gun hands lose their touch because they got too friendly with a bottle.' He motioned toward a chair. 'I never heard of you till you

15

came into the bar. I'd like to know a little more about you.'

'Not much to know,' I said. 'I used to live in Burns. My ma still lives there. I buckarooed for several outfits on the other side of the Blue Mountains. I've made my own living since I was twelve years old. I've killed a few men, mostly in Winnemucca when we made our fall drive. There's always a lot of hell raised down there at shipping time.'

He fired a cigar and sat down on the bed. He asked, 'You've never hired out as a gun hand?'

I shook my head. 'I'm a cowboy.'

I wasn't altogether lying. Just partly. What I didn't tell him was that a few small outfits would throw their herds together and drive to Winnemucca to the railroad. I was a cowhand, all right, but mostly I went along on those drives because I was good with a gun, and there was always trouble with the buckaroos from the big outfits when we hit town the same time they did. Three or four men were killed every fall in gunfights that we didn't start.

Dunn acted as if he didn't believe me. He had reason to doubt my word because most men who were fast with a gun were likely to hire out as fighting men and do as little range work as possible, partly because the majority were lazy when it came to hard work, but mostly because they didn't want to take any chances on getting their hands bunged up.

16

Dunn tongued the cigar to the other side of his mouth and asked, 'You got any objections to working as a gun hand?'

'No,' I said. 'Not if the pay's right.'

'I told you what we'd pay,' he said.

'That's good enough,' I said, 'but I'd like to know what the shooting's all about.'

'There ain't been any shooting yet,' he said, 'but it's likely to start in a week or two.' He took the cigar out of his mouth and rolled it between the tips of his fingers. 'We've got a problem in Wyoming that maybe you've heard about. The big outfits are being rustled blind. They're all going to be broke in a year or two if this keeps up, so we're fixing to do something about it.'

I'd heard of the trouble, all right, but a man hears all kinds of stories, some pitched one way and some another, all depending on the sympathy of the man telling the story. It would be this way with Dunn, I figured, and right then I made up my mind that I didn't want any part of this row.

'These rustlers are bunched in the northern part of the state,' he went on. 'It's good cattle country as long as the range is kept open. Of course that's part of the trouble. Homesteaders have been moving in by the hundreds. To make it worse, some of the cowboys have decided to try it on their own, so they take up a quarter section and claim they're in business, which I reckon they are.

17

With a running iron.'

'Don't you have any law in the country?' I asked.

He snorted a laugh. 'Hell yes, we've got law. Their law. We had our sheriff in office till the last election, but there were too many of them. They voted him out and put their own man in. Well, you figure out what's been happening since then.'

I still had no interest in the job, but the situation fascinated me. I'd often thought that if the little cowmen would get together, they could control local politics, but I'd never heard of them doing it. Now, from what he was saying, they had done the job and controlled the legal machinery of the county.

Dunn's cigar had gone out. He struck a match and held the flame to the cigar as he pulled on it. Then he said, 'We're going to bust up their politics. We'll make another county or two out of Mule Deer County, which is the one they've got under their thumb. It's a hell of a big county, too big for one sheriff to handle even if he's honest, which of course this one ain't.'

Dunn waggled a finger at me. 'You wouldn't believe how brave them thieving bastards are, knowing what their sheriff will do. A few days ago a rancher had just finished his spring gather and had started to brand when a band of rustlers rode up, pulled their guns on the men doing the branding, and took over the job themselves. I guess they branded four, five hundred calves, using their own brands, o' course, then they rode off, and do you think the sheriff would do anything? Hell no.'

I felt like laughing. This was my kind of fight, but I'd be on the other side, not Chauncey Dunn's. I almost told him I was heading for Mule Deer County in the morning and I'd be in the fight up to my neck on the side of the little ranchers, the men he was calling rustlers, but I didn't. I wanted to hear what else he had to say.

'Another man went to Texas to recruit some fighting men,' Dunn went on, 'and I came to Idaho and Oregon, but by God, I didn't find anybody who'd fit the bill till I saw you take care of the Harrigans. Right then I told myself you were my man if you were in the market for a job.'

He stopped talking and looked at me, waiting for me to say I'd take the job, but I didn't say it. Not then. Instead, I said, 'I still ain't sure just what your side is figuring on doing.'

'Why,' he said as if it was as plain as the nose on his face, 'we're gonna do the only thing we can. We're taking some men into Mule Deer County and we're hanging every damned rustler we can lay our hands on including the present sheriff. We've got a list of about sixty men who are known rustlers. With them out of the way, we'll break the back of the whole bunch. We'll get our own sheriff into office and there won't be no more stealing. Not of horses or cows. Or grass, neither.'

That staggered me. It was wholesale murder any way you looked at it. I knew what went on in a cattle country. If a man had a few head of cattle and was bucking the big outfits, he was a rustler. There was no such thing as a small honest rancher in the mind of the big cowman.

'What you're talking about is forming a vigilante committee,' I said.

'You can call it that if you want to.' He shrugged his shoulders. 'Why hell, man, if there hadn't been vigilantes in Virginia City, where would the honest, law-abiding people be? Or up there on the Yellowstone and the Missouri when Granville Stuart and his stranglers cleaned house? Yeah, you can call 'em vigilantes if you want to, but I'll guarantee one thing. When we get done, there won't be no more rustlers.'

I shook my head. 'I don't think you can do it,' I said. 'I don't know how big an army you're taking in, but you'll be outnumbered and you'll wind up dead.'

He grinned. 'No we won't. That's where we're playing it smart. They won't know what's happening until it's too late. Like I said, we're bringing in some men from Texas. There'll be some local men, too, but nobody's gonna talk about it. We'll move in fast and the job will be done before the rustlers know we're even in the country.'

Surprise! That was the key. It would work if the surprise was complete and the little cowmen didn't have a chance to get together. But suppose the surprise was not complete? The settlers would rise up like the colonists had back in 1775 and the invaders would be swinging from the limbs they planned to use for the settlers.

That was when the idea hit me. I could be the one to see that the settlers weren't surprised! I could take the job and go along with the invaders until we got close to Mule Deer County, then I could spread the alarm.

'Well, are you interested?' Dunn demanded.

The idea made me warm all over. For the first time in my life I had a chance to get back at not one big cowman, but a whole passel of them. It would be the biggest thing that ever happened in the West. I could see it in my mind, a limb holding a dozen of the biggest cowmen in Wyoming.

'Yeah,' I said, having trouble keeping the feeling of satisfaction that I felt from showing in my voice. 'I'm your man.'

He rose and held out his hand. 'I figgered you were or I'd never have made the offer.'

I rose and shook hands. 'When do we start?'

'We'll take the morning stage out of Delaney,' he said. 'We'll board the eastbound train tomorrow evening out of Baker City.

21

Leave your horse here. We'll furnish horses, saddles, Winchesters, and ammunition. We'll barely get to Cheyenne in time. It looked for a while like I'd come back empty-handed, but it's better to go back with one good man than none.'

'I'll ride out to the K Bar and draw my time,' I said. 'I'll come back and get a room here in the hotel and be ready to go in the morning.'

I kept that warm feeling all the way to the K Bar. From what I'd heard it was the big cowmen who ran the state of Wyoming. It would be their back that got broken, not the settlers. I'd never in my wildest dreams come up with anything like this. Chauncey Dunn was bringing in one good man, all right. A better man than he knew.

## CHAPTER FOUR

I tied in front of the K Bar ranch house and went in. Marge was in the kitchen, but as soon as she heard the front door, she ran into the living room, then stopped when she saw me and began to cry. I walked to her and patted her on the shoulder, awkwardly, I guess, because this was a new Marge. I hadn't supposed that anything this side of hell would break her up.

22

Suddenly she threw her arms around me and hugged me. 'Bruce, I didn't think you'd live to come back,' she said. 'I thought the Harrigans would kill you.'

'No, they're the ones who are dead,' I said. 'Quinlan won't bother you anymore.'

She looked at me for a long moment, swallowing and wiping at her eyes, then she said, 'I kept your supper hot for you.'

I followed her into the kitchen and sat down at the table. She dished up my food and took a chair across from me. She said, 'Tell me about it.'

I did, not mentioning Chauncey Dunn. When I finished, she said, 'I'm sorry I told you that you were fired. I guess you knew I didn't mean it.'

'I didn't figure you did,' I said, 'but I am quitting, now that your trouble is over. No reason for me to stay on here.'

'Oh, yes there is,' she said. 'You don't know how much I've been depending on you. You can't leave, Bruce.'

'You can always hire a thirty-a-month cowhand,' I said. 'I've got a job in Wyoming where I'll use my gun. The wages are a little better.'

'Bruce, you're not a killer,' she cried. 'You can't do that. I'll raise your wages.'

'Don't try to talk me out of it,' I said. 'I'm good with a gun. I'd be foolish not to take this job when I've got the chance.'

'I told you I'd raise your wages.'

'I'm getting one hundred dollars a month,' I said. 'You can't pay that and you know it, so quit trying to talk me out of it. I've made up my mind.'

'I'll make you my partner,' she said as if she were suddenly frantic about keeping me.

I went on eating, knowing I couldn't make her see it my way, so there wasn't any use talking about it any more. When I finished, I pushed back my plate and said, 'I'm staying in town tonight and I'm taking the morning stage to Baker City. I'd appreciate it if I could leave my gear here and you'd have one of the boys fetch my horse out from town tomorrow. I'll leave him in the livery stable.'

She didn't argue any more. She said, 'Of course. I'll get your money.'

She rose and went into her bedroom, returning a moment later with three gold eagles. She didn't owe me a full month's wages, but I took it, figuring I had earned it tonight. She followed me to the door, a glum expression on her face.

I pushed the screen back and stepped out on the porch. I said, 'I told Quinlan that I would hear about it if he ever bothered you again and I'd come and kill him. I will, too, and he believed me.'

'Bruce, Bruce, suddenly I wonder if I know you at all,' she said in a low voice. 'There's more important things in the world than killing

24

people.'

'Like working cattle for thirty a month and beans? No, I don't think there's anything more important than killing the right people.'

I had never told her about my childhood or why I hated big cowmen, and I wasn't going to now. Let her think what she wanted to about me. It probably wouldn't have made any sense to her anyway. She followed me out to my horse, not saying a word until I was in the saddle.

'Bruce, you've always got a job here as long as I own the K Bar,' she said. 'I'd like to talk to you about a partnership if you're interested. I never had a man work for me before I could really trust. K Bar will never be a big outfit, but it's big enough to give a living to both of us.'

I'd never thought much about my future, but what she said about the K Bar was true. I liked it here. I knew as well as she did that I wasn't a killer and I knew that I could get along with her. I also knew that the days when a man could make his living with a gun were numbered.

'I may take you up on that,' I said.

I rode away. I looked back once and saw that she was still standing there, a tall, stringy woman. The strength of the land was in her, and I don't think she would ever have caved in no matter what Quinlan said or did. I thought about it all the way to Delaney, and I never did

25

figure out why she had said she would take Quinlan's offer and move into Baker City.

I guessed Quinlan had returned to Horsehead. At least I didn't see him. In the morning I had breakfast with Dunn. When we finished, he gave me the one hundred dollars he had promised I'd get when I agreed to take the job. I felt a little guilty about taking it, knowing that I'd be selling this bunch out in a few days, but I couldn't turn it down without making him suspicious.

We arrived in Baker City in time to catch the afternoon eastbound train. I wondered about Dunn's place in this vigilante bunch, but I didn't get around to asking him until we were on the train. When I did ask him, he eyed me a moment as if wondering what business it was of mine.

Finally he said, 'I was commissioned to enlist some men who were good with their guns. I told you that. I just couldn't find 'em.'

'I know you told me that,' I said, 'but what I'm wondering is whether you're a stockman, or how you got on the side you're on.'

The corners of his mouth began to work and I could see the fury start to build in him. Then he burst out, 'Yeah, by God, I was a stockman in Mule Deer County until the rustlers stole my spread, but I'm gonna get it back and I'm gonna help hang every rustling son of a bitch we can find. Now are you satisfied?'

26

'Yeah, I'm satisfied.'

'All right, then quit asking questions,' he snapped. 'You're hired to fight. Just obey orders and earn your wages.'

'Sure,' I said. 'I was just curious.'

I put my head against the red plush back of the seat and thought about him saying not to ask questions. That was the way they were. They made all the decisions and the laws, and nobody was to ask any questions. The funny part of it was that they could hire all the men they needed to do their dirty work, men who obeyed orders and earned their wages, men who didn't have any stake in the game and didn't give a damn about how the fight turned out as long as they got their money.

The way he used the word rustlers made me mad. He had told me they had a list of sixty men they were going to hang. They didn't know these men; they didn't know for a fact they were rustlers. To their way of thinking, if a man was a small rancher, he was a rustler.

Then I thought about how it had been when I was a boy, and I thought of the men I had killed, men who obeyed orders and didn't ask questions and earned their money. Never once had I got the men who were responsible for the crimes that had been committed. It was like cutting off a few branches, but the tree was still there and still growing.

I said I'd tell you why I hated the big cowman. I guess there hadn't been a day since

27

it happened when I hadn't thought about why my father killed himself that evening on the Malheur. Some things you forget in time and some you remember, and this was one I remembered, even the smallest detail.

## CHAPTER FIVE

I was born in a sod house on a homestead in central Kansas. I lived in the sod house until I was ten years old, not out of choice, but because my father spent ten years trying to build that homestead into a farm that would give us a decent living. He failed, not because he was shiftless, but because of dry weather which meant no crop, or low prices which meant no money when we did have a crop.

My mother was a quiet, hard-working woman who never complained and had a talent for somehow making-do with what we had. I was born when she was eighteen, she was twenty-eight when we left the homestead, but she looked years older. If we had lived there another ten years, I suppose she would have died at the age of thirty-eight as many homesteaders' wives did, worn out by the demands that were made upon her.

My father was twenty-one when I was born, and so was thirty-one when we left. The hard work had not worn him down as it had my mother. He was a big, fine looking man, strong and competent. To me he was everything that a man should be and I worshipped him.

As soon as I could walk, I would follow my father around the farm as much as he would let me. When I was big enough to work, he gave me jobs that I could do and I never objected. Not that I liked to work. I was as lazy as the next boy, but I wanted to please my father, and I knew I wouldn't do that by shirking my work.

I was the only child. Something happened to my mother when I was born so she could not have any other children. She was unhappy about that, but I once overheard her say to my father that she was glad she didn't have eight children the way one neighbor family had, all of them half-starved and sickly and living in a kind of poverty that by comparison made our life seem one of riches.

Being the one child wasn't so bad, I guess. At least I always had enough to eat. Not much variety most of the time, but enough so that I was big and strong for a ten-year old. On the other hand I suspect I was spoiled, being the only child, and certainly I was the apple of my parents' eyes. I had all of their love, and I think that was not as good as having it spread among several children.

At any rate, we were a happy family for all of our poverty. I rode a pony to school which was three miles away. The teacher was a mean old bird, but I learned, and I'm grateful for that. We had church in the schoolhouse on Sunday morning. We had social gatherings there, a Christmas program and pie and basket socials.

The years on the homestead were good years and sometimes I wish we had stayed. I'm sure we would have been spared the tragedy that came to us in Oregon, but that was not the way it was to be. I learned at the age of ten to accept what comes and not waste time wishing it had been some other way.

My father was an ambitious man and the homestead frustrated him. He was confident that he could do anything in the world that he set his mind to, and after ten years he finally accepted the dismal truth that hard work was not going to put him ahead. One evening after supper he announced out of a clear sky that we were selling out and moving to Oregon. Good land was still available there, he said, and water was not the scarce commodity it so often was in Kansas.

My mother was shocked and cried a little, but I thought it was great. To my way of thinking, Oregon was out west, but Kansas wasn't. I started dreaming about the trip from the moment my father said we were moving.

It was a job to sell the homestead, and when my father finally succeeded, the amount of money he received was pitifully small, but it was enough, he said, to get us to Oregon. We set out in a covered wagon loaded with everything we owned. I rode my pony; my mother and father rode in the wagon, with our cow tied behind.

Actually the trip was uneventful, but my imagination gave it exciting events. This was long after the days when the long covered wagon caravans rolled across the plains, but I'd heard stories about them, so I imagined great herds of buffalo stampeding across the short grass and attacking Indians and fierce outlaws. With my father's help, I fought them off and was, in my imagination, responsible for their safe arrival.

In spite of the dust and thirst and the hard work of staying in the saddle all day and the thunder storms that turned the road into bogs, the trip gave us a great deal of pleasure, and I shall never forget the good times we had. My mother looked younger, it seemed to me, from the day we left the sod house. She sat on the wagon seat with her arm through my father's, listening to everything he said as if each word was a pearl of wisdom.

My father, who had been a silent man, became talkative, mostly about the great future that lay ahead for us, and the opportunities that waited for a man who was willing to work. I believed him and my mother believed him, and every day brought us a little nearer to the pot of gold that was just waiting for us to pick up at the foot of the rainbow.

The pot of gold became a little tarnished when we reached Boise because my father had a chance to talk to some people who had been in the Willamette Valley and had left. They said the good land in western Oregon had been taken years ago. The land that had been fertile forty years ago was worn out, they told him, and the good land that was left was covered with tall fir trees and it would take a life time to clear forty acres.

There was still good land to be taken in eastern Oregon, they assured him. Dry, sure, but there was water in the streams. When a man irrigated, he could be certain that a drought wouldn't hurt him. Don't follow the old Oregon Trail, they said, but go up the Malheur River. You'll find good land along it, or farther west around the little town of Burns, or even farther west near Prineville.

My father wasn't quite so exuberant after we left Boise. My mother and I both felt it, but we didn't mention it. This whole business was my father's idea and it was up to him to find a new home for us. He changed back and had his old enthusiasm after we crossed the Snake River and headed up the Malheur.

'Plenty of water coming down this river,' he said. 'We'll find some good land and stake out a homestead. I wasn't figuring on irrigating, but it's like they told me in Boise. We'd always have water this way and not have to be looking up at the sky every day to see if them clouds are just empties going by or if they're gonna give us some rain.'

I couldn't tell whether he was just trying to make us feel better, or if he really believed what he said. I didn't care much for the country. We were in a canyon a good deal of the time and more often than not it was rough going. I was hoping to see some mountains with big trees and lots of game, but it struck me that it was a dry, forlorn land and I guess I hoped he didn't find what he was looking for.

I had a hunch my father really didn't know what he was looking for, but he fooled me. We were out of Boise about ten days or two weeks when he had to leave the river and climb a long grade. When we reached the top, my father pulled the team up and just sat staring at the valley below us for about five minutes.

'Look at that,' he said. 'Just look at that. Did you ever see a purtier piece of country in your life?'

It did look good for a fact. The river lay a mile or so to the south, but a small stream came in from the north and ran the length of the little valley. I guess there was about a quarter section of good, level land below us with the greenest grass I had seen for a long time and a grove of big cottonwoods. Off to the north I could see some pine-covered mountains, so I figured there would be plenty of game up there. Maybe some fish down here in the creek, too.

'Well sir,' my father said, looking at my mother, 'I guess the Lord led us right to this valley. That's our home down yonder.'

'Do you think there's some reason it hasn't been homesteaded before this?' my mother asked.

'No, no,' my father answered. 'It's just that folks passing through here went right on to the Willamette Valley, but we're not going to do no such thing. We'll set up our tent and tomorrow I'll ride back to Vale and file on this valley.'

'We won't have no neighbors,' my mother said.

'We'll find some,' my father said. 'There's got to be somebody living around here.'

We went on down to the bottom of the grade and my father pulled off into the cottonwoods. We set up our tent and I gathered enough firewood for supper while my father took care of the horses. Later I walked down to the creek and looked it over. A fair amount of water was running in the stream, but I wasn't sure what it would be like later in the summer.

I returned to the tent and mentioned my doubts to my father. He just shook his head, feeling so good that nothing could take the big grin off his face. 'Don't you worry none about that, Bruce,' he said. 'That creek's gonna run all summer. Even if it don't we'll build us a dam up yonder where it comes out of the hills and make a reservoir that we'll fill when the creek's high and we'll have enough water to raise the best crops you ever seen.'

I still didn't like the feel of things. After supper I saddled my pony and rode upstream to where the creek came out of the hills. I found a bunch of cattle there, fifteen or twenty head, all branded XX. It was dusk when I got back to camp and told my father about the cows.

'Oh, pshaw,' he said, 'I was hoping there wouldn't be any cows around here. We'll just have to do some fencing. We've sure got to keep 'em out of our fields.'

He left the next morning as soon as he finished breakfast after telling me to put the day in gathering wood because, 'We're going to have to hustle to get a crop in this year. It may be too late now, but at least we'll get a garden planted and a few acres of oats for our horses.'

After he left, I said to my mother, 'I don't like it.'

'I don't either, Bruce,' she said, tight-lipped. 'There's something wrong with a good piece of land like this that's right beside the road and nobody has taken it, but your father can't see that yet.'

He was a mighty stubborn man, once he made up his mind about something, and he had fallen in love with this little valley, so nothing could change his mind. I started gathering limbs that had fallen from the cottonwoods and piled them a few feet from the tent.

Along about noon two men rode down the creek. I saw them as soon as they came out of the hills and ran and told my mother. She got the Winchester out of the wagon and stood in front of the tent until they rode up.

'Mornin', ma'am,' one of the men said. He nodded at me. 'Howdy, sonny.'

I said, 'Howdy,' but my mother didn't say anything. She just stood there, grim-faced, holding the Winchester on the ready.

The man who had spoken was a little man with a face as wrinkled as a prune. He looked old, but maybe the wind and sun had fried his skin and made him look old. His face had the leathery appearance that cowboys get, so I decided he wasn't as old as I'd thought at first.

The second man was younger with a round face and blue eyes. He was big, bigger than my father, and he had a funny grin on his face all the time as if he kept thinking of something funny that he knew but we didn't.

Both men carried Colts and both had rifles in their boots. The little man was the leader, or at least he did the talking. He looked us over, then studied the tent and the wagon, and finally pinned his gaze on the wood I'd piled up.

'I'm Hank Gibson and this is Smiley Rehn.' The little man jerked a thumb toward the big one. 'Who are you and where are you from?'

'Our name is Cassidy,' my mother said. 'We're from Kansas.'

'Where's your man?' Gibson asked.

'He went back to Vale,' my mother said 'He's going to file on this little valley.'

'I had an idea you were up to some foolishness like that,' Gibson said. 'I wish we'd got here sooner. I'd have saved him his time and trouble. You see, nobody's gonna settle here because this valley is part of the XX range, and we sure ain't fixing to let no sodbusters plow the grass under, so as soon as he gets back, tell him to move on.'

He nodded at Rehn and they started to ride off. 'Suppose we don't go?' my mother called after him.

They reined up and looked back. 'Why, ma'am, we'll kill your man,' he said in as matter-of-fact tone as if he was talking about killing a rooster for a Christmas dinner.

They rode away then. My mother stood looking at them for several minutes, then she said, 'So that's what's wrong with this valley.'


CHAPTER SIX

My father got back to camp at dusk the next day. We saw him riding down the long grade, and when he reached us, my mother was waiting for him in front of the tent. He had waved to us when he was still fifty yards away and we'd heard him whistling, so we knew he had succeeded in filing on the valley.

Before he could say a word, my mother cried, 'We've got to leave here. Now.'

He reined up and looked down at her, his expression one of complete bewilderment. He asked, 'What's got into you, woman? I filed on this quarter section. It's public domain just as I said it was. It's ours now.'

'Of course it's public domain,' she said, 'and Bruce and I know why it's never been homesteaded. I told you something was wrong with it.'

He stepped down, cuffed back his hat, and wiped the sweat from his forehead. 'So there's something wrong with it. Well, they sure didn't mention it at the land office.'

'Of course they wouldn't,' she said, and told him about Gibson's and Rehn's visit.

She gripped both of his arms as she talked, her face close to his. I had never seen her so excited or so worried, but when she finished talking, my father just laughed.

'So that's what's wrong with it,' he said. 'Well, I don't know anything about the men you're talking about, or the XX they work for, but I do know we're within our legal rights to claim this valley, and they ain't within theirs when they say they're gonna kill me because they don't want this grass plowed up. It's just a

38

bluff. I'm surprised you didn't see through them.'

'It's no bluff,' my mother said in a low tone, the excitement leaving her. 'Do you know what it would be like for me and Bruce to be left alone?'

He put his arms around her and kissed her. 'Yes, I know, and I ain't aiming for it to happen. I don't figure on giving up what's rightfully ours, neither. We can fight, too, you know.'

She whirled away from him, saying, 'Supper will be ready in a few minutes.'

He was puzzled. He shook his head, then he looked at me. 'Well, son, they must have given you and your ma quite a scare.'

'They sure did,' I said. 'They're bad men.'

'Then we'll have to be bad men, too,' he said.

There wasn't any more said about it that evening, at least not that I heard. But the next morning my parents looked as if they hadn't slept any during the night, and both were very formal and polite to each other. This was not their usual way and it bothered me.

As soon as we finished eating breakfast, my father said, 'Bruce, we'll get busy clearing the sagebrush off a piece of land so we can get a garden in. We'll study the creek and find a good place to take some water out, and then we'll decide where we want the cabin, but that'll have to wait a few weeks.'

We found a curve in the creek just above the tent that my father said would be a good place to start the ditch and we picked a nice, high spot about fifty yards from the creek for the house, then he got a pick and a couple of shovels from the wagon and we started digging some of the sagebrush out. My father kept the Winchester close to where we were working.

They came in the middle of the morning just as my mother and I knew they would. I'm not sure whether my father really expected them or not. He was always inclined to dismiss anything which happened to someone else and not take it seriously until it happened to him. Still, he did keep his rifle handy, so he had not entirely discounted what my mother had told him.

As soon as the two men came into view, I said, 'They're here.'

'I see them, son,' my father said. 'Don't pay no attention to them. Just keep on working.'

We did, but it was hard for me to do. I wanted to run away, to yell at them to leave us alone, to pick up the rifle and start shooting, just anything, but I didn't. My father had always been able to handle anything that came along, so I figured he'd handle this one. Well, I hoped he could, but I guess that down inside me I wasn't so sure.

Not a word was said until the XX riders were about twenty feet from us. Suddenly my father dropped the shovel, picked up the

40

Winchester, and lined it on the two men, the hammer back. They reined up and stared at him, surprised, I guess, that there was any fight in a settler.

'You men are trespassing on my land,' my father said. 'Now turn around and vamoose. This is my homestead. I filed on it yesterday.'

Hank Gibson thumbed his hat back and leaned forward. He said, 'Friend, I guess you didn't get the message we left with your wife yesterday. This ain't your homestead and it never will be. It's XX range and it's gonna stay XX range. You ain't plowing up no grass in this valley.'

My father didn't argue. He just raised the rifle and fired at Gibson. He aimed to miss him, all right, but it was too close for comfort, maybe a little closer than my father had intended for it to be. I think Gibson must have heard the bullet whisper in his ear. He didn't say a word. He just turned his horse and rode back up the valley.

Smiley Rehn said, 'You made a mistake just then, granger. It's always a mistake to shoot at Hank Gibson and not kill him.'

He turned around and rode after Gibson. My father put the rifle down. He was trembling and a muscle in his cheek was jerking the way it did when he was either so mad or so scared that he didn't know what to do. I hadn't seen it happen very often. He picked up the shovel and started to dig at

41

another clump of sagebrush.

About five minutes passed before he could say in a normal tone, 'They won't be back.'

I was proud of my father, but I was also scared. My mother was, too, though she didn't come out to where we were working. When she called dinner, we went down to the creek and washed, and when we got to the tent, she said, 'I guess you know now I didn't make that story up.'

'I knew you didn't,' my father said. 'It just wasn't anything to get worked up about the way you did.'

She threw up her hands. 'I don't know what it would take to convince you. They'll come back and they'll kill you.'

'No they won't,' he said. 'I told you it was just a bluff. Now that they know we ain't running, they'll let us alone.'

That was the first time, I think, that I understood the truth about my father. He was so stubborn he was foolish. I was only ten years old, but I knew they'd be back, and my mother, who wasn't used to facing situations like this, knew they would be back. My father did, too, with his rational mind, but he wasn't listening to his rational mind. Still, he did listen enough to take his Winchester when he left camp to milk the cow.

He had tied the cow about fifty yards above the tent near a patch of willows. He laid the rifle down and had taken about three squirts of milk when Gibson and Rehn slipped out of the willows, each holding a gun in his hand.

My father fell away from the cow the instant he saw them and grabbed for the Winchester, but he couldn't get it. Gibson fired, the bullet kicking up a little geyser of dirt between my father's hand and the rifle.

'You ain't getting the drop on me again, granger,' Gibson said in the coldest, meanest tone I ever heard. 'Now stand up and let your pants down.'

My mother ran out of the tent when she heard the shot.

Gibson yelled at her, 'Go back in, ma'am. This ain't gonna be nothing for you to see.'

She turned and ran back into the tent. My father just stood there, staring at Gibson, and for the first time in my life I saw fear in his face, the kind of fear that makes a man a shadow of himself.

Gibson said, 'By God, you heard what I said. Let your pants down. It's gonna be tough on you when you do what I say, but it'll be a hell of a lot tougher if you don't do what I say.'

'What . . . are . . . fixing . . . to . . . do?' my father asked, his voice breaking.

'He wants to know what we're fixing to do, Smiley?' Gibson said. 'Get out your knife. This knife has cut a lot of calves, granger. I reckon it can do the same for you. We figure to geld you in case you still ain't figured it out. One thing we can't stumick is a fiesty granger. I reckon you won't have no more fight in you after we get done.'

My father was shaking. He dropped to his knees. 'Don't do it,' he begged. 'Please don't do it. We'll leave in the morning.'

Rehn had taken his knife from his pocket and had opened it. Now he ran a finger along the edge of the blade. 'It's sharp, granger,' he said, 'so it won't hurt much, but you sure ain't gonna be no good to your wife from now on.'

'No,' my father screamed. 'Please! We'll do anything you say. Please don't do it.' His teeth were chattering. Spit dribbled down his chin. He held out his hands in a begging gesture. 'Please.'

Gibson stood with his gun pointed at my father's chest. He winked at Rehn. 'Ain't he the tough one now? He's like the rest of 'em. Put him in a corner and he caves in.'

'On your feet, sodbuster,' Rehn said. 'We ain't got all day. Get them drawers down.'

I had moved around until I stood over the Winchester. They weren't watching me, or I didn't think they were. I stooped and picked it up and lined it on Gibson, but I was too slow. Rehn was on me before I could pull the trigger. He hit me across the top of my head with the barrel of his six-shooter. That was all I knew. I guess that if I hadn't had my hat on, he'd have cracked my skull wide open.

I must have been out cold for a long time. When I came to, it was dark. I heard my mother crying. My head was splitting and I couldn't stand up. I tried, but my knees gave under me and I fell down. I crawled to her, and in the moonlight I saw that she was cradling my father's head on her lap. I pulled at her sleeve, but it was a long time before I got her attention.

'What's the matter with him?' I asked.

She turned her head and wiped a sleeve across her eyes. She whispered, 'He's dead. After they left, he shot himself through the head.'

## CHAPTER SEVEN

We buried my father on the slope above the tent. We didn't dig a very deep grave, but it had to do because we weren't able to do any better. We didn't put up any kind of marker except to pile up some rocks at the head of the grave.

By the time we finished it was so late in the day that we decided to stay there another night. We knew Gibson and Rehn might return and kill us, but I guess neither one of us cared very much right then. The sky had fallen on us and we didn't know what we'd do. There wasn't much money left. All we had were the wagon, the team, my pony, the cow, and the stuff we had in the wagon.

We hadn't said much all day, but that night after supper my mother said, 'Well, Bruce, you're going to have to be the man of the family.'

'I will,' I said.

'We'll go to Burns tomorrow,' she said. 'No use going back to where we came from.'

'I'll get a job,' I said.

'You'll do no such thing,' she said sharply. 'I'll get the job. You're going to school.'

I didn't argue. I very seldom argued with my mother. She was kind and soft and I thought very pretty, considering the way we had always lived, but there was something else about her. When you pushed the softness back so far, it stopped, and if I kept on arguing, it was like ramming my head against the side of a cliff, so I had learned long ago not to push that far. I didn't mention what I was going to do when I got a little older. I was going to kill Hank Gibson and Smiley Rehn.

We pulled down our tent in the morning and loaded the wagon, then harnessed the team and hooked up. I tied our cow behind the wagon, but we didn't start for a little while. My mother just stood there looking at the grave and then up and down the valley before she climbed to the seat.

'I guess there are more broken dreams lying around in the West than any other place in the world,' she said.

I handed her the lines and mounted my

46

pony. We didn't travel very fast or very far that day, or on the following days, either. We had enough grub in the wagon to last for several weeks and I shot a couple of jack rabbits.'

We pulled into Burns late one afternoon and made camp at the edge of town. After we'd set up the tent and had finished supper, we explored the town. That didn't take long because Burns wasn't much of a town.

The buildings were frame. In some places there were boardwalks and in other places there wasn't anything but a dirt path, so I figured that it would be a muddy job walking through town after a rain. Main Street wasn't much, either, just a wide patch of dirt with a lot of wheel tracks and hoof prints and horse droppings and sagebrush.

A few men were standing on the boardwalk staring at us with ill-concealed curiosity. Several horses were tied at the hitch rails and the saloons were going full blast. We walked rapidly past them, my mother wondering aloud if there were any decent women in town. If there were, they were at home and not on the street.

If we were going to work, and I hadn't given up the idea that I could get a job, it seemed to me we'd better keep going to the Willamette Valley. At least a lot of people lived there, and where there were people, there would be jobs. I couldn't see any chance of either of us getting a job in a little cowtown like this, and I said so.

'We'll be in no hurry,' my mother said, and I felt that toughness in her again, so I shut up.

One store was open. Kimbroe's General Merchandise. My mother stopped and stared at the sign above the door, the letters faded, every i dotted by a bullet hole. Then she shut her eyes and stood motionless for a full minute. She opened her eyes and said, 'We'll go in here.'

My mother always claimed that she was guided when it came time to make decisions. She never said how she was guided or who was doing it, so I never understood how it worked. I wasn't even sure what she meant, but I did know there had been a few times when it had worked, and this was one.

It was dusk now. There was a lighted wall lamp in a bracket that gave out a dim light on one side of the store. The interior smelled musty, and even though I wasn't an expert on housekeeping, it seemed to me there was no order in the store and more dust on the counter and floor than there should be.

A man was eating supper at a desk in the back of the room. My mother walked up to him, her shoulders back, her head high, and asked, 'Are you Mr. Kimbroe?'

'Yes.' He put his fork down and chewed for a moment, then he asked, 'What can I do for you?'

He was sixty or more. He had a kindly face,

48

but he looked tired and beaten down. Even frail, I guess, and I thought that maybe he just didn't have the strength to keep the store up the way he should.

'Mr. Kimbroe,' my mother said, 'I am young and strong and I need work. You need someone to help you in the store. I want you to give me a job.'

He laughed. It wasn't a good sounding laugh, but a kind of sorry sound as if there wasn't anything humorous in the whole wide world, or maybe he was laughing at himself and the notion that he could give a job to anyone.

'Ma'am,' he said, 'you are right that I need someone in the store. If you know of anyone who will work for nothing, then I would be pleased to give him a job.'

'I will work for nothing,' she said. 'I mean, no money. Are you married? Do you have any children?'

'I have no wife and children,' he said, 'and if you don't want money, just what do you want?'

'A place for us to live,' she said, 'and food to eat. I will keep house for you and I will work in the store in my spare time.'

He poked a boney finger at me. 'This your boy?'

'Yes,' she said. 'He's all I've got. My husband was murdered about a week ago.'

'I'm sorry, ma'am,' he said. 'Mighty sorry.' He rubbed his chin and looked at me and then at my mother, and finally he added, slow-like as if he had to think out each word, 'We'll give it a try. Just in the store at first. Do you have a place to live?'

'We can stay in our wagon,' she said.

'Good,' he said. 'You can come to work at eight o'clock tomorrow morning.'

It worked out. I don't know what led her to that store or why she stood out there in front with her eyes closed, but I do know she hit it off with Kimbroe right from the first. About a week later he said we could move into his house, which was just back of the store. We did. The house was a mess, but we cleaned it up until it had a shine to it I'll bet it hadn't had for years.

I found plenty to do around the store. One day Kimbroe said to my mother, 'That's a good boy you've got there, Mrs. Cassidy. He's a worker.'

'Yes,' she said. 'My husband taught him to work, but as soon as school starts, he's going to school.'

'Of course,' he said. 'A boy has to have some schooling.'

His trade picked up, too, after people found that the store had been cleaned up. I don't think he was sick. I guess he was older than I had thought at first and he was just worn down to a nubbin. Anyhow, he was tickled that more customers were coming in and he gave my mother credit for what had happened.

'I guess you were sent from heaven, Mrs. Cassidy,' he said. 'I don't know what's the matter with me, but I'm too tired all the time to do anything. I just wasn't taking care of things proper.'

He wasn't so tired after we had lived with him for a while. He said my mother's cooking was responsible. I think it was, too. He added several pounds and his face looked younger, and he did more work around the store until there wasn't much left for me to do.

I started school in fall, and after I had a few fights to show the other boys that nobody was going to run over me, I got along fine. The next summer I got a job in the hotel because I wasn't needed in the store. I didn't get paid much, but it was better than nothing.

There was always something doing around the hotel. The Prineville stage stopped there and new people had rooms there, the drummers particularly, and usually some of the old-timers were lined up in the chairs on the porch smoking and whittling and yarning, and it was fun to sit out there and listen to them.

The main reason I wanted to work there was the nagging memory that I'd made myself a promise that I'd kill Hank Gibson and Smiley Rehn when I got older, and I figured I was old enough to do it. Sooner or later, if they came to Burns, they'd show up at the hotel. The following summer Smiley Rehn did.

51

# CHAPTER EIGHT

The day I saw Rehn was one I'll never forget. It was late in July, a hot day, I remember, and when Burns had a hot day, it had a corker because there weren't many trees in town and no green grass to speak of, so there was nothing to break the sunshine. It just hammered down at us and bounced off the dry earth, hotter than when it came down.

Some of my chores in the hotel were not exactly fun jobs like emptying the spittoons and the slop jars. I didn't mind using the broom and the mop so much. I did a little bit of everything that was of a cleaning nature, so I had the run of the place, even the bar, though neither the owner nor the bartenders would let me hang around there. Usually I'd go into the bar in the morning and empty the spittoons and not go back in until the following morning.

On this particular day I had gone to supper. I didn't always return to the hotel after I'd eaten, but there wasn't anything to do in the store or in the house, so I wandered back to the hotel. I might say I was guided to go back the way my mother would have said, but I guess no divine power was going to guide a boy to kill a man.

I had a hunch when I saw the XX horse tied

in front of the hotel. This was a big bay gelding. I couldn't remember just then what the horses looked like that Gibson and Rehn had been riding that day, but in the two years I'd lived in Burns I'd seen mighty few XX horses, so this one made me stop and think.

I finally dredged up a mental picture of Rehn's horse. He was riding a bay gelding. I guess I stood there about five minutes studying that horse, and the longer I stood there, the more certain I was that he was Rehn's horse. Then my heart began to pound.

When I went into the lobby, I sneaked a look at the register and saw that Smiley Rehn was down for Room 22. I walked over to one of the black leather chairs that was set back in the corner behind some geraniums and sat down. I was trembling. This was my chance, but I didn't know how I was going to do it or even if I could.

While I was sitting there Rehn came out of the dining room chewing on a toothpick. He glanced at me and right then my heart dived clear down into my boots. I figured he'd know me, but he walked on past me into the bar. I should have known he wouldn't recognize me. I had grown a lot. Besides, he probably hadn't paid much attention to me anyhow. To him a kid was just a kid.

I sat there for an hour or more, I guess. It was black dark by that time and I didn't see any more of Rehn. Suddenly I was scared.

Even though he had paid for a room, he might have decided to head back to the XX. I got up and went into the bar, pretending I was checking on the spittoons. The bartender started yelling at me to get the hell out of there.

For a moment I didn't see Rehn because he was bellied up against the bar at the far end talking to a couple of buckaroos from the P Ranch south of Burns. As soon as the bartender started bawling me out, I figured it would call Rehn's attention to me, and it did. I just about fell on my face when he called, 'Kid! Hey, Kid!'

Naturally I figured he had either recognized me or saw something familiar in my looks. For an instant I was tempted to cut and run, but right away I knew that would be worse than bluffing it through, so I walked up to Rehn and looked him in the eye, asking, 'What do you want, mister?'

He was smiling the way I remember him, but he didn't look quite right. Then I realized he was drunk. Not falling-down drunk, but he'd been putting the whisky down pretty good judging from the almost empty bottle on the bar.

He had trouble talking, but he managed to say, 'Put my horse up, kid.' He fumbled around in his pocket and pulled out a four bit piece and tossed it to me.

'Which horse is it?' I asked.

54

I saw then that he wasn't in shape to recognize me or anybody else, so I quit worrying about it. He said, 'A bay. Only XX horse out there.'

'Sure, mister,' I said. 'I'll take care of him.'

It took me about ten minutes to go to the livery stable and get back. I stopped outside and stared through a window long enough to see that Rehn was still bellied up against the bar. Right then it came to me how I would do it.

There was a back stairs that led from the alley to the second story of the hotel. I climbed it and walked along the hall to Room 22, then slipped into the room across from it. That room was vacant and no one was likely to check in this late at night, so I figured it was safe to hide there.

I didn't have to wait more than an hour until Rehn staggered up the stairs and along the hall, weaving from side to side. He stopped in front of Room 22, fumbled around trying to find the knob, then finally gripped it and turned it. He pushed the door open and went in.

I had opened the door of the room where I was hiding just enough to see what was going on. Rehn had left his door open. I waited a few minutes, then slid into the hall and saw that no one was in sight. I went into Rehn's room and shut the door, then I leaned against it, my heart hammering so hard that it seemed it would jump out of my throat.

It's a funny thing how you anticipate something for a long time the way I had anticipated killing Rehn and Gibson, but it's different when the time comes to actually do it. I wasn't backing out, though. I didn't even think of doing that.

Rehn hadn't bothered to pull his boots off. He had simply fallen across the bed on his belly and started to snore. I'd heard him before I came into the room. Now his snores seemed louder. He turned on his side, then went on over and lay on his back. The window had no shade or curtain, and with the moon being full, quite a bit of light was falling into the room.

I eased over to the bed, stopping each time a floorboard squealed, but it wouldn't have made any difference if I'd jumped up and down. Rehn was long past the point of hearing anything. I slipped my hand into his pocket. His knife was there. I pulled it out and opened the long blade. For a moment I stared at it in the moonlight, feeling dead sure this was the same knife he had used on my father.

I raised the knife and gripping it with both hands, drove the blade into his chest as far as it would go, then I turned and ran. He made some sounds, I guess. I'm not really sure. All I wanted was to get out of there. I made it to the alley door, glanced back and didn't see anyone, then I went down the stairs and ran home.

In about five minutes I was back in my own bed. I went in through the window as I often did when I didn't want to disturb my mother or Kimbroe. My mother always looked in on me before she went to bed. I hadn't been back in my room three minutes before she came in, holding the lamp high so the light fell on my bed. She left when she saw I was there, closing the door behind her.

I had trouble sleeping that night. Not that I had any remorse. I felt no more guilt than I would have if I'd stepped on a fat bug. Smiley Rehn was the kind of man who should have been killed a long time ago. If he had, my father would have been alive. No, I got to thinking that maybe one stab wound wouldn't kill him. I would be mighty sorry if I'd missed my chance. I wished I'd hit him another lick or two with that knife.

I didn't need to worry. The next morning at breakfast Kimbroe told us what had happened. Someone had found Rehn dead in his bed. It didn't take long for that kind of news to spread around Burns. Nobody could understand it, but folks knew that the XX had run roughshod over a lot of people and half the men in Burns might have had reason to kill Rehn.

The sheriff asked a lot of questions, but he never suspected me, being only a kid, and no one else did, either, so the murder was never solved. I'm not sure about my mother. She might have suspected me, but she never gave the slighest hint if she did.

I stayed in Burns for another month, but after fixing Smiley Rehn, I had to get out. I was big for my age and strong, so folks took me for two or three years older than I was. I knew I could make out, so I wrote a note to my mother telling her I loved her, but it was time for me to go and I knew she would be all right, working for Kimbroe.

I left in the middle of the night, taking a few dollars I'd saved, a change of clothes, and a sack of grub. I rode out of town, headed west, and kept going until I got to Crooked River where I got a job on a ranch as a chore boy. I suppose my mother wasn't really surprised because a lot of boys ran away from home and she knew I was getting antsy and had reached the place where I had to be on my own.

Later I came back to Harney Valley and worked for some of the little outfits. One man I worked for was an old Texan who had been handy with a gun when he was younger and he taught me all the fancy tricks that a gun artist uses.

Not many men in Oregon were familiar with these stunts. Most of them were for showoffs and I never was a smart alec, so I doubt that many people around Burns knew how fast I was. They did in Winnemucca, though, so I suppose the stories got back to Burns.

I saw my mother often while I was working

in Harney Valley. She married Kimbroe and I was glad because he was good to her and she'd have a home as long as he was alive. Once she told me that Kimbroe would never take my father's place, which I knew, but Kimbroe was an easy man to be around and I think my mother was reasonably happy. I lost my job and drifted north to Baker County looking for work, and that was how I hooked in with the K Bar.

## CHAPTER NINE

We reached Cheyenne early one morning. Chauncey Dunn hurried me off the train and into the rear coach of another one that was waiting on a siding. I didn't even have time to ask questions about why we were in such a hurry or why all the windows were shaded on the coaches of the waiting train. One thing was sure. No one who was outside could look through the windows and identify anyone who was inside the coaches.

The car was filled, but apparently Dunn didn't know any of the men. He almost ran down the aisle, glancing to one side and then the other, but he didn't speak to anyone or even nod. As for me, my first reaction was that I had never seen as tough looking men in my life as this bunch was.

59

I'd heard of Texas gunmen, but I didn't think any of them ever got to Oregon, and I was sure I'd never seen any. Most of these men were young and most were wearing showy clothes. They looked at us curiously and exchanged grins and winks, but none of them said anything that I heard. It was just as well because I was on the prod before I'd gone halfway down that aisle.

We went on into the next car, Dunn saying something over his shoulder about wanting me to meet Major Lew Walters. He was in the next car along with half a dozen other Wyoming cowmen. It was like a breath of fresh air to see these men. Talk about a different breed of dogs than the Texans. They were much like the Oregon stockmen I had known. Richer, maybe, but very much like them.

Dunn introduced me to each man. I judged that Major Walters was the leader and he was the only man I was disappointed in. He was short, maybe five feet six or seven, and he wasn't big. He might have weighed one hundred thirty-five pounds, but he had quite a belly. Somehow the leader of a Wyoming vigilante group having a potbelly jarred on me.

Walters shook my hand, his gaze slowly moving down the length of my body and then back again. He nodded approvingly. 'You'll do, son,' he said. 'Looks like you might have come right off our range.'

'You've got some Oregon cattle on your

range,' I said. 'Maybe you've got some Oregon buckaroos, too.'

'Maybe,' he said, 'though we've got Texas cattle on our range, but our cowboys don't look like the men in the back car.'

'They'll do their part,' a man named Yancey said sharply. 'You were prejudiced from the minute you saw them, Major. That's not fair.'

'I'm sorry,' Walters said, and his voice changed so it had a steel edge to it and right then I raised my opinion of the man. 'My prejudice ain't important. The only important thing is whether they'll fight and obey orders. That's up to you, Slim.'

Yancey lowered his gaze. 'They'll fight, Major. I'll guarantee that.'

'But you won't guarantee they'll obey orders?' Walters asked.

'Well no,' Yancey admitted. 'I'd say it depends on the orders. They're a mighty independent lot.'

'They're your responsibility,' Walters said shortly. 'You recruited them.'

A man who had been introduced as Dr. Orr said, 'I don't agree to that, Major. We'll hang together or we won't hang at all. I'd say the responsibility belongs to all of us. If we've got some gunslingers here who won't take orders, we'd better stop this thing right now.'

Walters was troubled. He took several seconds to bite off the end of a cigar and light it, then he said, 'I reckon you're right, Doc.

61

We'll have a talk with these men. We can't call this affair off, but we sure as hell can let any of them go who don't savvy our organization.'

'And have 'em ride on north to Mule Deer County and pass the word that we're coming?' Yancey shook his head. 'We can't do that, either, Major.'

'We'll go talk to 'em,' Walters said. 'Come on, Slim. The rest of you stay here.' He nodded at me. 'Cassidy, you can ride in this car.'

'Thanks,' I said. 'I sure ain't in favor of riding with the Texans.'

They were back in about five minutes, both men looking glum. I had a notion they hadn't fired any men, but they hadn't been satisfied, either. I sat down in a seat and kept my ears open, but nothing much was said. A minute or so later the train began to move and we were on our way. As soon as we were out of Cheyenne, the order came back along the aisle for us to raise the shades.

We were headed for Casper, Chauncey Dunn told me, but it sure took a long time to get there. I don't know how many stops were made. I lost count long before we got to Casper, but there were a lot of them. Men and horses were taken on at every stop. These men were cowhands and foremen and owners, and again I had a feeling that they were no different from the buckaroos I'd worked with in Oregon.

Doc Orr rode beside me part of the way. He was an affable man and I liked him right off. He owned a ranch east of Cheyenne, he told me, and he hadn't suffered from the rustlers' raids, but the expedition needed a doctor and he'd volunteered.

'I've had my doubts about the wisdom of this venture,' he said in a low tone. 'Maybe we can clean out the rustlers, but even if we do, we may turn public opinion against us.'

'Most cattlemen don't give a damn about public opinion,' I said.

He nodded agreement. 'That attitude is a mistake. We've run things in this state back in territorial days and we still run things, but it won't go on forever. Some of the state can be used for farming, and we're getting more and more homesteaders who are going to try it.'

'Trouble is,' I said, 'a lot of grangers can't tell the difference between land that can be farmed and land that ain't good for anything but grass.'

He snorted. 'You're sure right on that. They hurt us whenever they plow up grass on range land. They'll starve out, but meanwhile they've ruined that much grass. It will take a long time to come back.'

He filled and fired his pipe, then he said moodily, 'I don't like the cut of the jibs of these gunhands.' He motioned toward the back car. 'I've been through a couple of range wars and I have no use for men who make a living by hiring out their guns.'

'I don't, either,' I said, thinking of Hank Gibson and Smiley Rehn.

He shot me a quick glance. He said, 'But that's what you're doing.'

I guess I got a little red in the face. I couldn't, of course, tell him why I was here, so I shrugged and said, 'You got me there, Doc, but I'm a working cowhand and a good one. I doubt that there's a man in the back car who ever earned a nickel working cattle.'

'You're right on that,' he said. 'I didn't peg you as being the same caliber as the Texans. It struck me queer when you made that remark.'

'I've got reason to feel the way I do,' I said, and told him about my father. I added, 'I guess that's why I hate professional gunmen. That's what Gibson and Rehn were. The XX hired them to keep homesteaders off their range and they weren't expected to do any work.'

'It's an old story here in Wyoming,' he said. 'The only difference is that we've been pushed to the wall and that's why we're doing this. I figure that if the rustlers can set up their own government and elect their county officials in Mule Deer County, they can do it in Albany or Laramie counties, or any of the others.'

We didn't say anything for a time, then we talked about cattle and prices and weather. Presently we ran out of things to talk about. He rose, saying he'd see me later and walked down the aisle and sat down beside a man who had just gotten on the train at Chugwater.

Later, Dunn came by and sat down beside me. He motioned to the men in the car who were sitting in front of us. He asked, 'You feel at home with these men?'

'Sure,' I answered. 'Didn't you feel at home in Baker County?'

'Yeah, I did,' he admitted. 'I guess I hadn't thought about it any other way, but I see what you're getting at. Well, I didn't cotton much to the idea of recruiting men from other states, but the Major and some of the rest claimed we couldn't raise enough men in Wyoming. I still think we could.'

There was a diner on the train. We had our dinner and later the Texans came through our car on their way to the diner. I didn't pay any attention to them as they went by and when they came back, I was asleep.

The afternoon dragged by, the train moving by spurts and jumps just as it had that morning. We ate supper and returned to our car and the Texans went by again. This time I paid a little more attention to them.

Several wore two guns. One of them, a slim, lanky kid not out of his teens, wore pearl-handled guns. He walked with a kind of swagger which I couldn't entirely blame on the train. I spotted him when they came back. He wore a skimpy mustache which was more peach fuzz than whiskers, but I guess it was the best he could grow. He had several large

65

pimples on his face which didn't add much to his appearance.

There was something else, too, a kind of arrogance that set my teeth on edge. He gave me a long look as he walked past me. It was more than arrogance. It was plain insolence. I figured he was the kind who would shoot a man and enjoy doing it.

Then I sat up, a prickle running down my spine. A little man had just come into the car. I always took a second look at little men, but I didn't need a second look at this one. He was Hank Gibson. I recognized his ugly face the instant I saw it.

## CHAPTER TEN

I slept very little that night. It wasn't that I couldn't sleep on the train because I had slept pretty well on the long trip from Baker City to Cheyenne. It was Hank Gibson. He had never been out of my mind for any great period of time after my father's death.

I had settled half the debt when I had killed Smiley Rehn, but ever since I had done that, I had been constantly prodded by the other half until I had almost decided that this hell would last a lifetime, that I would never see Gibson again. Now I had seen him, I knew where he was, and I had no intention of letting him get away, but just how was I going to handle it?

If I killed Gibson, I might have to take on forty Texans. I might even get into trouble with Major Walters and the rest of the Wyoming bunch. Well, these were chances I would take. I couldn't risk letting Gibson get away from me.

By the time we reached Casper the following morning, I had decided that I'd jump Gibson the first time I caught him away from the others. I didn't have to wait long. There was a lot of confusion when we unloaded.

The men who had joined the expedition after leaving Cheyenne had their own horses and saddles. The rest of us had to be outfitted. Along about the middle of the morning I saw Yancey lead a roan gelding to Gibson. They talked for a while, then Gibson led his horse to a pile of saddles, picked one up, and saddled the animal.

I moved toward Gibson, knowing that Chauncey Dunn would find a horse and saddle for me. There was no hurry about that. Gibson paid little attention to me. He mounted and trotted the horse the length of the train and back. He reined up and stepped down, then stood patting the horse's neck and talking to him.

No one else was around. I walked up to him and stopped about twenty feet from him. I said, 'Gibson.'

He wheeled away from the horse and

glowered at me. He snapped, 'What the hell do you want?'

'I'm going to kill you,' I said.

He laughed. 'I doubt that,' he said, 'unless you shoot me in the back, which same is probably what you're fixing to do.'

'I won't do that,' I said. 'Do you want to know why I'm going to kill you?'

He shrugged his shoulders. 'It makes me no never mind. There's men all over the West who want to kill me and some have tried.'

'I want you to know why I'm killing you,' I said. 'You remember working for the XX with Smiley Rehn?'

'Sure I remember,' he said impatiently. 'Nothing unusual about it. I've had jobs like that in a dozen places.'

'You remember a family of a father, a mother, and a ten-year-old boy?' I asked. 'You and Rehn gelded the father. He killed himself that evening. The law would never hang you for murder, but that's what it was, so I'm going to execute you.'

'You're the kid?'

'I'm the kid,' I said. 'Two years after it happened I killed Rehn with the same knife he used on my father.'

He stood motionless, staring at me. He hadn't taken me seriously before, but he did now. I have no idea what went through his mind or what made him decide to have it over with. Maybe he was afraid I would shoot him in the back. Anyhow, he was standing there staring at me one minute, his hatchet of a face knotted up in a scowl, and the next minute he was going for his gun.

I don't know how many men Gibson had faced and killed. Maybe he had done his killing by shooting men in the back as he had accused me of scheming to do. In any case, he wasn't very fast with his gun, not nearly fast enough.

He had his gun out of leather and almost leveled when I shot him between the eyes. I couldn't have done much better if I'd measured the distance across his face and marked the spot.

For a few seconds the confusion and the hurrying around and the shouted curses all came to a stop as the men turned away from what they were doing to see what the shooting was about. When they saw what had happened, they started toward me, the Texans in the lead. I backed up against the rear coach, my gun still in my hand.

For a little while I had the feeling I was going to take on the forty Texans. I'd have killed some of them, all right, and they surely would have killed me. The pimply faced kid with the pearl-handled guns was in the lead, but it was my good fortune that Major Walters was the closest man to me and Slim Yancey wasn't far from him. They were the first to get to me. They faced the Texans, Walters raising both hands.

'You can stop right where you are,' Walters said. 'One killing is enough.'

'Not near enough,' the pimply faced kid said. 'One killing calls for two, the second one being a hanging.'

'We'll find out about the first one before there's a second one,' Walters said. 'Now get back to what you were doing.' He motioned to the kid. 'Rio, get your hand away from your gun.'

'No, by God,' the kid said coldly. 'Step away, Major. You, too, Mr. Yancey. If this yahoo wants a gun fight, I'll give it to him.'

'No,' Walters said. 'There's been some question about whether you men would obey orders. Now I'll tell you how it is. We don't want any men in this party who won't obey orders. Men like that endanger the whole venture. Now decide which way you want it. Either you do what I say and you do it pronto, or get over there into the depot and wait for the next train back to Texas.'

They stood with their legs spread, several with their hands splayed over gun butts, all of them letting me know they hated me with a passion. Slowly the pimply faced kid dropped his hand to his side.

'All right, Major,' he said. 'I'm obeying orders. Now let's see what you do with this killing son of a bitch.'

Walters turned to me. 'What happened,

Cassidy?'

'I was talking to him,' I said, 'and then all of a sudden he drew on me. What was I supposed to do, stand here and let him kill me?'

I had no intentions of telling them why Gibson drew on me. The fact remained that Gibson had been the first to go for his gun and all I could do was to hope that someone had seen it from the first.

'He's a liar,' the kid said. 'Nobody could beat Hank Gibson to the draw if he had an even break.'

'Did you see it?' the Major asked.

'Sure I seen it,' the kid said, 'I was standing yonder. This bastard pulled first.'

Doe Orr had been standing to one side watching and keeping out of trouble. Now he walked up to Walters. He said, 'The Kid is the one who's lying. He was standing yonder all right, but his back was to Cassidy and Gibson. I was watching the whole business. Cassidy walked up to Gibson and started talking. The talk didn't last long until Gibson went for his gun.'

Orr turned to the Kid. 'You were dead wrong about nobody beating Gibson to the draw. Cassidy did it. I've seen a few gun fights and I never saw a faster draw in my life. If I were you, I wouldn't try pulling against him.'

The Kid didn't say a word. He stood there fuming until Walters said to me, 'I guess nobody can blame you for defending yourself.

71

Rio, you and Buel there take the body to the undertaker. We'll be moving out in an hour or so. You can catch up with us.'

Still the Kid didn't move for several seconds, then he said to me, 'I'm going to kill you. I don't know when or where, but I'll do it.'

'Now is as good a time as any,' I said.

He didn't answer. He wheeled away and got Gibson's horse. His friend Buel joined him. Together they lifted the body to the saddle, lashed it down, then rode toward town. The Texans broke up, but Doc Orr remained beside me until we were alone, then he asked, 'Was Gibson one of the men who ruined your father?'

'He was,' I said. 'I've been looking for him ever since, but I never saw him from that day till last night when he walked back through our car from the dining room.'

'Quite a coincidence,' Orr said, 'him showing up with this bunch of Texans.'

I shook my head. 'I don't think it's much of a coincidence. I knew he'd been fired when the XX changed hands. The new owners didn't figure to operate the way the old ones did, so Gibson probably drifted to Texas where he'd be most likely to find the kind of job he wanted, then when Yancey showed up recruiting gunhands, Gibson threw in with him. Gunfighting jobs are pretty scarce these days.'

Orr nodded and scratched his cheek. He

said, 'Well, that sounds reasonable, all right. Now I've got one piece of advice. Watch your back. The Rio Kid is a bad one.'

'I aim to,' I said.

I didn't tell Orr I wasn't going to be with the outfit very long. If I hadn't had reason to pull out before this, I did now. The Rio Kid or some of the other Texans would see I got a dose of lead poisoning the first time we had a fight. Besides, I didn't have any use for an outfit that would hire men like the Rio Kid. But this was beside the point. I was here to see that a bunch of big cowmen got their necks stretched and that was still what I aimed to do.

## CHAPTER ELEVEN

We didn't get away from Casper until afternoon. We only traveled ten miles that day. I didn't know how far Mule Deer County was from Casper, but I did know it was a long ways, and at this rate we'd take a week or more to get there. We were held back by the chuck wagon, and by our late departure, but mostly, I think, because Major Walters and the others who were in charge just didn't seem to be in any hurry.

The whole business got crazier by the hour, at least to my way of thinking. If I'd been in Major Walters' position, I wouldn't have taken the chuck wagon. I'd have had each man tie a few days supply of grub behind his saddle. I would have been out of Casper by at least ten o'clock that morning, and I'd have set a good, fast pace.

That evening I stuck pretty close to Walters and Dunn and Doc Orr, figuring that if I wasn't careful I might not live long enough to reach Mule Deer County if one of the Texans got a chance to slit my throat. That evening after supper Walters took a folded sheet of paper from his pocket and went over a list of names with Dunn and Yancey and Orr.

I pretended that I wasn't paying any attention to their talk, but the truth was I was straining both ears as hard as I could. I gathered that the list named the marked men. The ones I heard most often in the conversation were Red Dawson and Peewee Curry. I'd never heard of either man before, but apparently they were well known in Wyoming.

'I aim to put the ropes around the necks of those bastards myself,' Chauncey Dunn said in a passionate voice. 'They stole my cattle and kept on stealing until they broke me. I got no help whatever out of the God-damned sheriff in Jackson. Nothing.'

'The sheriff ain't gonna get nothing out of us, either, except a rope on his neck,' Yancey said. 'He's the first man we'll hang when we get to Jackson.'

'If I could name one man who was responsible for this state of affairs,' Walters said, 'it'd be Sheriff Abe Hogan. He's given every sodbuster and renegade cowbody license to rustle all the cattle and steal all the horses he wants, and then protect their stolen property after it's stolen.'

'As long as they steal from the right men,' Dunn said. 'That's the hell of it. They never steal from each other. They just steal from men like me who brought the first herds into the country and started ranches.'

'It's anarchy,' Doc Orr said. 'Just plain anarchy.'

I had to admit that if I had been in Chauncey Dunn's boots, I'd probably feel the same way he did, but my boots were of a different size. I would have felt a little more sympathy with Walters and Dunn and the others if they had some semblance of legality on their part, but to go in this way with a bunch of Texas gunmen to hang the men they had on their list without even a pretense of a trial was vigilante law at its worst.

The venture was headed for failure. It couldn't be any other way. It was my guess that they'd hang a few men, but as soon as the word got around Mule Deer County that this was happening, the invaders would find themselves in a hornet's nest.

The men around the fire were still talking when I drifted off to sleep. My last thought was that I'd see to it that the sheriff in Jackson heard about what was going on and that would make failure certain.

We traveled farther the next day, but we didn't break any speed records. That evening Major Walters told Dunn to take another man and ride ahead in the morning and do some scouting. Walters said he had heard that Dawson and Curry had bought a spread on one of the forks of Powder River.

'If that's true,' Walters said, 'you get the place located for us and we'll nail those two sons of bitches on our way north.'

'I know where it is,' Dunn said, 'but I'll find out if they're living there. It ain't much out of our way.'

Dunn and another man pulled out at dawn the next day. Walters still didn't seem to be in much of a hurry. By evening we were in Mule Deer County and I began to worry that I wouldn't be the one to take the news to Jackson.

Somebody else headed north would be bound to see us and make a good guess about what was happening. A party as big as this one wouldn't be riding toward Jackson just for the fun of the ride, but apparently this didn't occur to Walters.

That night the Rio Kid and his friend Buel caught up with us after we'd made camp. They reported to Walters that Hank Gibson had been properly buried in Casper. I was standing beside Walters while the Kid gave his spiel, but he ignored me. I might as well not have existed. That wasn't natural.

After the Kid and Buel left to join the rest of the Texans, I said, 'Major, do you know what's going to happen to me the first time that we run into any powdersmoke?'

He nodded. 'Doc told me why you went after Gibson. I'm not blaming you, Cassidy, but I think you're foolish to stay with us. You'd be safer back in Casper. Keep the advance pay that Chauncey gave you.'

I shook my head. 'I won't quit yet. I'll just try to stay out of their way.'

'It won't be easy,' Walters said. 'Nobody's gonna blame you if you pull out. It was unfortunate that Gibson was with us, but of course that was something you couldn't have foreseen.'

It was plain enough that he wanted to get rid of me, but I wasn't ready to go yet. I said, 'If it gets too rocky, I'll pull out.'

He let it go at that, but I could see he wasn't satisfied. After I went to bed that night I thought about what Walters had said, but I couldn't figure out what was in his mind. The more I thought about it, the more certain I was that he really wanted me to leave. He certainly wouldn't object when I did ride out, though he would object if he knew what I intended to do, which same, of course, I wouldn't be telling him.

The only reason I could think of that he didn't want me to stay with them was that he was afraid there would be more dissension and he didn't want that. He knew that as long as I was around, the Texans would be proddy and hard to get along with.

I finally decided that it was Walters's own weakness that was responsible for what he'd said. He didn't have the guts to fire either me or the Texans, but I was the easiest to get rid of. If I didn't leave of my own choice, he'd get around to firing me.

It was late before I went to sleep. I had barely dropped off when Dunn rode into camp. His talk with Major Walters woke me.

'Curry and Dawson are there, all right,' Dunn said. 'It's the old Anchor T spread. They've bought it and they're running about two hundred head of cattle.'

Walters snorted. 'Stolen cattle.'

'Probably some of mine,' Dunn said. 'It ain't much of a spread as far as buildings go, though they've got some good range including summer range in the Big Horse. I mean, all the buildings they've got are a small log cabin and a shed. A couple of corrals. Not much meadow land for hay, neither.'

'Hell, we don't care what kind of a spread they've got.' Walters was pulling on his boots. 'Out with it, man. Just what have you got on your mind.'

'I left Dusty there so we'll know if they're

78

still at their ranch,' Dunn said. 'What I had in mind was that we ought to ride out now. We've wasted too much time. If we don't get a move on, every man and his dog in Mule Deer County will know we're here. If we start now, well get to the Anchor T before sunup. We can nab Dawson and Curry while they're still asleep, hang 'em, and move on to Jackson.'

'All right,' Walters said. 'That's what we'll do. Slim. Doc. Cassidy. We're moving out. You boys wake everybody up.'

'What about the chuck wagon?' Dunn asked.

'It'll catch us at the Anchor T,' Walters said.

We had a job getting the Texans out of their blankets. I never heard so much grumbling in my life. It must have been after midnight before we got underway. The moon was nearly full so there was plenty of light to see where we were going.

I rode at the rear of the column and swallowed a lot of dust, but I preferred that to riding in front of the Texans and have one of them shoot me in the back. I figured something like that was due to happen and I'd made up my mind that it was about time to pull out.

The weather had been pleasantly warm all the way north from Casper, but now it turned cold. Two or three hours after we started clouds moved down from the Big Horns and covered the moon. Then the Texans began to curse. No one had expected a cold spell this late in the spring, particularly the Texans who were not used to spring storms. At least the cold got their minds off of me.

The first sign of dawn was in the eastern sky when the order came back along the line to dismount and leave the horses here at a line of brush along a small stream that apparently flowed into the fork of Powder River which was to our right. We'd move up on foot and there was to be no shooting until Walters gave the order. Doc Orr came back to the rear of the column, saying he'd been ordered to stay with the horses.

Orr recognized me in the thin light and said, 'You stay with me, Cassidy. Let the Texans do the killing.'

'Suits me,' I said. 'I reckon they won't need us. Seventy against two ain't bad odds for our side.'

Orr shoved his face up close to mine and peered at me as if trying to see what was on my mind. He asked, 'Are you thinking the same thing I am?'

'What's that?'

'That this is murder,' he answered in a low tone.'

'That's exactly what I was thinking,' I said. 'Why did you join up with this outfit if that's the way you see it?'

'I wish to hell I knew,' he said grimly. 'Right now it wouldn't take much to make me pull

80

out.'

'Me, neither,' I said.

Right then I knew that with Doc Orr in charge of the horses I'd have no trouble leaving when I decided the time was right.

## CHAPTER TWELVE

I guess we had been there about an hour before it was full daylight and Doc Orr and I could see the cabin distinctly from where we stood. Still there was no sign of life and I began to wonder if Dawson and Curry were there. I also wondered what Walters was waiting for.

It would be simple enough to move in and capture the two men if they were still asleep. But then I was done trying to figure Walters out. To my way of thinking the expedition had been badly led from the beginning and what was happening now didn't change my opinion.

Finally Doc Orr burst out, 'What in the hell are they waiting for?'

None of the others were close enough to hear me, so I said, 'Walters isn't my idea of a general. I've wondered about his title of major. What did he do to earn it?'

Orr laughed shortly. 'He was corporal in a Kansas regiment that did its fighting in Missouri and Arkansas. He's about as much of a major as I am.'

'Why was he picked to lead this outfit?'

'Two reasons. The first one is that he picked himself. He wanted the job and he's on good terms with the other cowmen of the state. The second one is that he's a rich man and put up most of the money for the venture. Well, maybe not most of it, but a big chunk anyhow.'

We didn't see or hear anything of the Texans who were hiding in the brush along the creek, or anything of Walters and the rest of the Wyoming men who were in the shed and corrals. The cabin didn't have either a window or door on the sides that were in our line of vision. It would have been easy to reach it without being seen by the men inside, but apparently that wasn't the plan. By this time I wasn't even sure there was a plan.

Presently we saw a column of smoke rise from the chimney and a moment later a small man came into view headed for the creek, a bucket in his hand. It would be Peewee Curry, I told myself. From what I'd heard, Curry was a small man and Dawson a very large one.

Curry had not taken more than three steps from the moment I first saw him before the Texans cut loose. Rifle fire blasted from all along the creek. The roar was deafening and for a moment a cloud of powdersmoke blotted out the scene before us. When it lifted, we saw Curry lying in the grass as motionless as a rag doll, the bucket on the ground beside him.

'My God,' Orr muttered, 'they never intended to take those men out and hang them. They just aimed to smoke them down in cold blood.'

Just then a big man who had to be Red Dawson darted into view, grabbed Curry by the shoulders and hauled him back around the corner of the cabin. It was one of the bravest acts I ever saw a man do.

I guessed the Texans were as surprised as I was. There were a couple of belated shots that were fired about the second he disappeared. As soon as he was out of sight, the whole bunch cut loose as if to make up for having missed him when they had a chance to kill him.

I couldn't tell from where we were standing how solid the cabin was, but it seemed to me that with that many men firing at it, some bullets were bound to get through the chinking and sooner or later Dawson would be hit.

I'd seen a man murdered and I would swear to it in court if it came to that. It was what I had come for. Now it was time to go. I was aware that Orr wasn't standing beside me as he had been. I looked around and saw that he had moved back about ten feet. He was sick. Right then I knew he was the wrong man for the job just as Walters was the wrong man for his and I guess Orr realized it, too.

He straightened up and wiped a sleeve across his mouth. He tried to say something but he couldn't make the words come out. He wheeled around and headed back along the line of horses to where his was tied near the far end. Mine was on beyond his. I caught up with him, asking, 'You had enough?'

'I've had a bellyful,' he said. 'You can take that two ways.' Slobber started running down his chin. He wiped it off with his sleeve. 'Funny about this kind of business. You don't really know what it's going to be like until you see it happen. I'm not sure that Walters ever gave the order to shoot. Maybe the Texans just cut loose. If they did, after Walters telling them not to fire until they were told to, then they're just as hard a bunch to handle as we figured.'

'Walters and Yancey and the rest will be sorry they ever recruited them,' I said. 'A small, fast-moving column of Wyoming men would have done the job better.'

We had reached Orr's horse, He stopped, looking hard at me, then he said, 'The Major told me you would be leaving on account of you figured the Texans would shoot you in the back the first chance they had.'

'That's right,' I said.

'Then you won't try to stop me from leaving?'

'Stop you?' I laughed. 'Hell, I'm going with you.'

'Then saddle up,' Orr said. 'Maybe I'm too late now, but I'm getting out before the law hangs me. That was murder, Cassidy. Curry was a rustler, all right, but shooting him down

84

that way was murder.'

I moved on to my horse. Orr started saddling his just as a man stepped out of the brush along the creek. He asked, 'What're you up to, Doc?'

'Some of our horses got away,' Orr said, making an effort to sound casual. 'I guess the shooting boogered them. I'm going after them.'

'You're lying, Doc.' The man pulled his gun. 'Some of us figured you had a yellow streak down your back. You ain't pulling out. Nobody is. We're into this together and that's the way we're gonna stay. Now pull that saddle off your horse. Say, where'd Cassidy go?'

I'd slipped up behind him, thinking this might happen. Before he could turn, I hit him across the top of his head with my gun barrel. He went down without a sound. I said, 'Let's move, Doc. Some of the others may be thinking the same way.'

A minute or so later we rode across the creek so that the brush would be between us and the rest of the party, then we busted the breeze getting out of there. After a while we slowed down, figuring they weren't coming after us.

Orr said resentfully, 'I don't have a yellow streak down my back. I've just come to my senses. That's all.'

I didn't argue with him, though I couldn't help wondering why he had volunteered to join this outfit. I couldn't believe that he was so lacking in imagination and foresight that he didn't know what was going to happen. If he hadn't volunteered, Walters or some of the other leaders would have found another doctor. Now they didn't have any.

Well, it was his problem and he had to live with it if he had a ranch in Wyoming as he had told me he had. Other stockmen would make it hard on him and I had a hunch he'd be selling out and leaving Wyoming.

'I'm turning north,' I said. 'I guess you'll be heading for Casper.'

His mouth dropped open and he stared at me blankly as if he couldn't understand why I was traveling north. He blurted, 'Why in the hell are you going that way? The only safe route is south. We'll catch a train in Casper.'

I shook my head. 'Doc, I'm not looking for a safe route. The only reason I let Dunn recruit me was so I'd have a chance to warn the settlers and it's time I was doing it. I can't stick with this bunch any longer.'

'Cassidy, for God's sake,' he burst out, 'you can't do a thing like that. If they're warned, all the damned rustlers and horse thieves in Mule Deer County will be on the prod and Walters and his men will walk into a trap.'

'That's the way I figure it,' I said. 'Ever since Dunn told me what the plan was, I've been dreaming of seeing about fifty big cowmen swinging from the limbs of a row of trees. It was the big cowmen who killed my father, not just Gibson and Rehn who used the knife. Catching up with Hank Gibson was a dividend I didn't expect. It had nothing to do with my joining the invasion.'

'Cassidy,' he said harshly, 'you are a God-damned traitor. You let Dunn recruit you when all the time you intended to sell 'em out.'

'That's right,' I said. 'Now if you're going to Casper, you'd better be on your way. I don't aim to let you shoot me in the back.'

'I won't let you do this,' he said angrily. 'By God, they've got to have a chance to clean up this mess. I'm going to make you come with me.'

'Doc,' I said, 'you're in no position to preach to me about being a traitor, not after the way you went off and left 'em without a doctor. If you think you can make me do anything, you're dead wrong. It's dangerous to try.'

I put my hand on the butt of my gun and nodded at him to tell him to go ahead and draw if he aimed to stop me. His face turned a sickly green. He didn't say a word. He just turned his horse and rode away. He didn't even look back. I waited for about three minutes until I was sure he wasn't going to try something foolish, then I headed toward Jackson.

The more I thought about him cussing me out and calling me a traitor after the way he had run out on Walters and the others, the madder I got until it became a fist-sized burr under my blanket. I finally decided the cowboy who had accused Doc Orr of having a yellow streak down his back was right. He wanted the rustlers destroyed, but he didn't have the guts to help do the job. Right then I decided I wouldn't have traded places with Doc Orr for all the cows in Wyoming.

## CHAPTER THIRTEEN

I rode hard until dark. By that time I was dog tired and so hungry that my stomach felt as if it was a great, empty hole in the middle of my body. I didn't know where I was going. The country didn't change, the Big Horns rising on my left and the plains rolling out to my right. All I knew was that somewhere to the north was Jackson, the county seat of Mule Deer County, and I had to find it.

About an hour after dark I saw a light ahead and figured I'd come to a ranch. I had no idea whether it was a small outfit whose owner would feel the way I did, or whether it was a big spread with an owner who would be sympathetic to the invaders. It was a question I couldn't answer, but I figured I had to get something to eat. Too, I figured I'd better find the answer to the question before I told the rancher where I was headed and why.

I reined toward the light. When I reached the yard, I called, 'Hello the house.'

For a moment nothing happened, then the door was yanked open and a man slid out fast, a rifle in his hand. He stood with his back to the wall beside the lighted doorway. For a moment he didn't say a word. I couldn't see him, but I knew he could see me.

'Who are you?' he asked finally.

'My name's Bruce Cassidy,' I said. 'I'm headed for Jackson, but I had to stop. I ain't et for a long time.'

'You alone?'

'I sure am.'

'Where you from?'

'Baker City, Oregon.'

'You're a long ways from home.'

'That's right,' I said. 'It's longer than I figured when I started.'

He was silent for a time and I began to think he was going to tell me to be on my way, then he said grudgingly, 'Come on in.'

I tied at the hitch rail and walked toward him, being careful to keep my right hand away from my gun. He was jumpy. That was plain enough from both the questions and his tone of voice.

When I reached the porch, he said, 'Go on in.'

I stepped into the house. A woman was standing beside the range. She was young, but the mark of hard work was already on her. She was scared. That was easy to read in her face. A couple of little kids, a boy and a girl, were hanging to her skirt.

The house was a log cabin, a single big room except for a curtain that closed off one end. I guessed that it partitioned the bedroom from the rest of the cabin. A table in the middle of the room was set for supper. Meat was frying on the stove, so I judged they were about ready to eat.

The man followed me in and closed the door. He looked me over carefully, still holding the rifle on me, and I looked him over just as carefully. He wasn't over thirty, partly bald, and very thin, with lines in his face that came from weather or worry or both. Like his wife, he was worn down to a nubbin by hard work. It struck me that there must be an easier way to earn a living for a family than what he and his wife were doing.

'You mind taking off your gun?' the man asked. 'You look honest enough, but we're expecting trouble and we're a scared bunch right now. If you're a stranger, you probably ain't heard.'

Normally I would never have unbuckled my gun for anyone, but I figured the man was harmless. He certainly wouldn't hurt me in front of his wife and children. Besides, I was mighty damned hungry, so I stripped off my gun belt and hung it and my hat and coat on the antlers near the door.

The man took a long breath and put his rifle down. He said, 'That makes me feel better. If you were here to do us any hurt, I knew damned well you wouldn't take your gun belt off.' He nodded at his wife. 'Put another plate on the table.' He held out his hand. 'I'm Jake Herder. This is my wife Effie and my children, Betsy and Hank.'

I said, 'Howdy.'

Mrs. Herder nodded and tried to smile, but it didn't come off. She was still scared. The kids peeked at me around their mother, still hanging to her skirt as if it offered an island of safety. I thought again this was a hell of a way to live, working themselves to death and being scared to boot.

'I just got in,' Herder said. 'I only own fifty head or so, and they've eaten about all that's fit to eat around here, so they started to drift. If they'd got as far as Arrowhead Range, that damned Yancey and his bunch of hardcases would have stolen every one of 'em.'

Surprised, I blurted, 'Yancey? Slim Yancey?'

'That's him,' Herder said in a tired voice. He motioned toward a bench along the wall. It held a basin and a bucket of water. 'Go ahead and wash up. Hank, how about you? Your hands clean?'

'He's ready to eat,' Mrs. Herder said tonelessly.

I washed and sat down at the table, prickles running down my back. I figured from what I'd heard that Slim Yancey had a spread around here, but I didn't know where. Now I was close to it and I'd have to ride across his range to get to Jackson.

Maybe it didn't mean anything, but his crew would be there and they might have orders to pick up every stranger who showed up on Yancey's grass. If they caught me and held me until the invaders got there, I'd be in one hell of a tight spot. Maybe I could get across his range before daylight. I'd better, I told myself.

Herder sat at the head of the table, his wife across from him. The boy was beside me, the girl across from me. Herder asked a blessing, then he passed the platter of steak to me. There wasn't anything else on the table except coffee and a plate of biscuits.

'Enjoy your steak, Cassidy,' Herder said. 'It came off the best Arrowhead steer I could find. That's the only thing we can thank Yancey for. We've been eating his beef regular, and I miss a few steers that I figure he fed to his crew. Only thing is he can afford to lose a critter now and then, and I can't.' He chewed a moment, his gray eyes fixed on me, then he said casually, 'You sounded surprised that Slim Yancey's spread was around here.'

'I was,' I admitted. 'I've heard of him, but I had the notion that all the ranches around here were small outfits like yours.'

He tried to grin, but his lips just wouldn't respond. There simply was no humor in the

92

man. I guess it had been beaten out of him by hard work and fear. His children reflected the way he felt. Neither one had said a word since I'd come into the house.

Mrs. Herder ate with her head down as if she was too frightened to look up. I kept thinking that it was a hell of a way to live, and then it occurred to me that probably most of the small ranchers in Mule Deer County lived the same way, at least since the rumor of the invasion had spread.

'I know,' Herder said. 'That's what the big bastards want all outsiders to think. You know, that they've been stole blind and they had to get out of the county. It ain't so, but they keep putting stuff like that in the newspapers, especially the Cheyenne papers where they spend most of their time.'

He took a drink of coffee and put his cup back on the table. He said, 'Now you take Yancey. He's been gone quite a while. He's been living high on the hog in that fancy club the cowmen have while his men do the work. He's here mostly just in the summer and fall when the weather's good. I used to work for him, so I know.'

It was time to bring everything out into the open. There wasn't any question about where Jake Herder stood, but I didn't know how he'd take it when I told him I'd been with the invaders. He might not believe my story, but then Sheriff Abe Hogan in Jackson might not, either. He might throw me into jail on general principles, once I admitted joining the invaders.

This was a possibility I had not thought about when I took Dunn's offer, but it had been nagging me ever since I got on the train in Cheyenne. Well, it had been too late then to do any good. It was like a lot of my best ideas. They came too late.

The steak was tough and took some chewing. When I got my mouth empty, I said, 'You were jumpy when I rode up. You said something about expecting trouble and since I was a stranger that maybe I hadn't heard. What'd you mean?'

Mrs. Herder looked up. She said sharply, 'You've been talking too much, Jake Herder.'

'Maybe,' he said. 'Maybe not. I don't peg this man for a stock detective. If he ain't, he can't hurt us. Anything I've said to him I'd say to anyone.' He turned to me. 'You know how it is with women, Cassidy. They scare easy.'

'Maybe she's got a right to be scared,' I said. 'You ain't told what it was I hadn't heard.'

'The story's out that the big cowmen are bringing in a bunch of hardcases to hang some of us,' he said. 'We've been watching for them. I've even heard they've got a list of men they're after so they know exactly who they're gonna hang. I figure I'm near the head of the list if they do have a list, living this close to Yancey's spread and eating his beef. You see,

94

that's a crime, but his eating mine ain't a crime. He figures everything I've got is his.'

I realized the story was out about the invasion, but I didn't know that the list of marked men was known. I asked, 'You got any way of warning folks when the hanging party shows up?'

He nodded. 'Two of the toughest and best fighting men we've got own a little spread south of here. They'll be the first to see the invaders and they'll warn us.'

'Red Dawson and Peewee Curry?'

He was surprised that I knew the names. 'How'd you hear about 'em?'

Instead of answering him, I said, 'They won't be warning nobody. I saw Peewee Curry shot to death and I figure that by this time Red Dawson is dead, too.'

'The hell!' Herder almost choked on the bite of meat that was in his mouth. 'How do you know about this?'

I told him. He sat there staring at me, chewing and swallowing. Before I finished, he began to shake. When I got done, he said in a low tone, 'Then they'll be here any time.'

'I don't think so,' I said. 'Walters ain't much of a hell-for-leather general. They've been taking their time right along, so I don't see any reason to think they won't go on taking their time. Chances are they'll stay the night down there at Curry's and Dawson's place. Chances are they'll eat supper and breakfast in the morning before they head on north. They'll want a night's sleep, too.'

'That's more'n we're gonna get.' He shoved his chair back and rose. 'We're going to Jackson and tell the sheriff the same story you just told me. Effie, as soon as it's daylight, you put some grub together and take the kids up to the line cabin. They won't bother you there. Stay till you hear from me. Come on, Cassidy. Let's ride.'

I wasn't done eating, but I saw it was all I was going to have unless I got mean and I didn't want to do that. I rose. I said, 'Thank you for the meal, Mrs. Herder. Good-by, Hank. Good-by, Betsy.'

The children glanced up from their plates, saying nothing. They just stared at me. Mrs. Herder stared at me, too, and didn't open her mouth. It was a hard, unblinking stare, bitter and fearful, as if she still didn't trust me. I turned, put on my coat and hat and buckled my gun belt around, and left the house. A few minutes later I was riding north again beside Jake Herder.

## CHAPTER FOURTEEN

Herder spoke only once on the long ride to Jackson. It must have been after midnight when we reined up to blow the horses. I saw a collection of lights off to the east and said that it was funny that anybody would be up this late.

'That's Yancey's Arrowhead,' Herder said. 'You can see anything around there. Men come and go all night long. I used to think he was in cahoots with outlaws, but I know that ain't true. It's more likely the gunmen he's hired to scare the rest of us and sometimes kill us. Take the sheriff who was in office before we elected Abe Hogan. He used to come out there often to talk to Yancey. Nothing but a damned paid dry gulcher.'

For a moment he was silent, then he went on bitterly, 'The big outfits have nobody to blame but themselves for any trouble they've had. A lot of the little fellows are like me. We used to work for Yancey or Chauncey Dunn or some of the others, then there was the Big Die and several years of low prices, so they let a lot of us go. We could ride out of the country and look for work somewhere else, or we could try to make it on our own. They wound up blackballing most of us who tried to start our own spreads. Now we can't work for nobody but ourselves.'

Again he was silent, brooding over old injuries, I guess. Finally he said, 'They've murdered several of us. Just last Christmas a young rancher named Bud Delong drove into Jackson to buy presents for his wife and kids. Some son of a bitch hid under a bridge. Just after Bud drove over it, this bastard shot him in the back. The team went on home and Mrs. Delong found Bud dead in the rig with blood all over the presents. It don't take much of that to turn us mean, Cassidy. I'll tell you one thing, Walters and his bunch are gonna find more trouble than they're looking for.'

We rode on. I tried to put it together, how men like Yancey and Walters and Dunn, who seemed decent human beings, could hire dry gulchers to murder young Bud Delong. Or, for that matter, hire men like Hank Gibson and the Rio Kid and murder Peewee Curry and Red Dawson. I couldn't do it. Anyway I looked at it, I couldn't make it sound like common sense.

When I first signed on with Dunn I had had visions of seeing rows of big cattlemen hanging from the limbs of cottonwoods like ripe fruit. It still might happen. The murder of Curry and Dawson would simply add fuel to the fire that had been smoldering here in Mule Deer County for a long time.

For some reason that eluded me I did not find any satisfaction in the vision of rows of cattlemen hanging from the limbs of cottonwoods. Probably it was because I knew some of the men who would hang and I didn't want to see it happen. They simply were not the devils with horns that I had always considered them. Maybe even the man who had owned the XX and had hired Gibson and

Rehn might have been decent enough if I had known him as I knew Dunn and Walters and Yancey.

Well, there was no clear answer to the problem. For the first time in my life I could see two sides to the question. Still, the invaders were dead wrong and I did not regret what I was doing. If the people of Mule Deer County could be warned and their lives saved, then I was doing a good thing. Whatever destiny lay ahead for the invaders was a fate they had brought on themselves.

We topped a ridge a little after sunup and looked down into a small valley that held the town of Jackson. A tree-lined creek bisected the settlement. It would, of course, head in the Big Horns and flow on out into the plains and probably empty into Powder River.

As we trotted our horses down the slope, I began to see the pattern of the town which was little different from other towns I had seen. There was the usual variation in houses, some frame, a few fine ones made of brick, and many log cabins, most of them small with dirt roofs. The business block was across the creek. The stores and offices were on one side of Main Street, a two-story frame courthouse on the other. Behind it was a log jail.

Something was going on. I was surprised, particularly this early in the morning. We crossed the bridge spanning the creek, the horse's hoofs making a pistol-sharp sound in the thin morning air. By the time we reached the business block, I guessed that someone else had brought the news ahead of me.

A burly man with a star on his shirt was in the middle of the street in front of the courthouse yelling orders. A dozen or more horses were tied at the hitch rails. Several men, eight or ten, were milling around the big man. Others were riding into town. One store, it looked like the largest in town, had lamps lighted inside and the front doors were open. A man I judged was the owner was passing out Winchesters to anybody who wanted one.

I said to Herder, 'They've already got the word.'

He nodded. 'Looks like it.'

He reined toward a hitch rail and stepped down. I turned in beside him, dismounted, and tied. Herder led the way to the big man with the star.

'Sheriff Hogan, I want you to meet Bruce Cassidy,' Herder said.

Hogan looked me over and held out his hand. 'Pleased to meet you, Cassidy,' he said. 'If you're looking for something to do, we've got a job for you.'

'He's got something to tell you,' Herder said.

'All right, out with it,' Hogan snapped. 'Hey, Aldrich, find Hoover?'

'Yeah,' a man answered who had just run across the courthouse yard. 'He'll be along.'

'This is important, Sheriff,' Herder said. 'Damn it, I want you to listen to what he's got to say.'

'I said to go ahead,' Hogan snapped.

'I saw Peewee Curry shot to death yesterday morning,' I said. 'By this time I'm sure Red Dawson is dead, too.'

Hogan stared at me blankly for a moment, then he grabbed me by the shoulders and shook me. 'How did you happen to be there to see it and how in the hell do you know Dawson's dead?'

'A party of invaders have come into the county,' I said. 'They're led by Major Walters. They came north from Casper. They've got a list of names of men who live in this country. They call 'em rustlers and they aim to hang or shoot all of 'em. Dawson and Curry were on that list. So are you.'

'By God, I asked how come you know so much about all this?' Hogan bellowed, and shook me again.

I jerked loose. 'There's about seventy-five men in the outfit,' I said. 'Slim Yancey has been in Texas recruiting gunmen. I'm guessing there's about forty of 'em. The rest are Wyoming men, some cowboys, but mostly they're owners and foremen. Yancey and Chauncey Dunn are two of 'em I know. Doc Orr was with 'em, but he vamoosed after he saw Curry shot.'

'Cassidy,' Hogan said, so angry he began to

tremble, 'if you don't answer my question . . .'

'All right,' I said, 'but I thought you ought to know what was happening. That's more important than how I happened to know all of this.'

'We've already heard, God damn it,' Hogan said, exasperated. 'Jinglebob Turner was riding past Dawson's and Curry's place when he heard the shooting.'

The men had made a circle around us. Now one of them said, 'That's me. Sounded like a battle. I didn't stop to see what was going on because when they spotted me, they started shooting at me, so I lit a shuck out of there. I couldn't see how many there were, but I'd say there were at least seventy-five.'

'We've known this was coming for a long time,' Hogan said, 'so they haven't surprised us, but we expected Dawson and Curry to warn us. We never figured them bastards would stop and waste a day just to get Dawson and Curry. You can be sure of one thing, Cassidy. We'll have more'n a hundred men blocking the road if they come past Arrowhead.'

'I didn't see the list,' I said, 'but from the talk, I got the notion that Dawson and Curry were Number One and Number Two.'

'And I'd be Number Three,' Herder said bitterly.

'And me Number Four,' Jinglebob Turner said. 'I'm surprised they didn't send some men after me.'

Suddenly Hogan remembered that he still didn't have the answer to his question. He grabbed me again by the shoulders and shoved his face close to mine. 'Now you're gonna tell me how you know so damned much about this business, Cassidy, or I'll throw you into the calaboose and let you rot there.'

He was a brutal-looking man, about fifty, I judged, with the biggest neck I ever saw on a human being. He had an underslung jaw and a pug nose and pale blue eyes set astride the bridge of his nose. I knew I was in trouble. He wasn't a man to listen, mostly because he had a one-track mind and right now that track was occupied by another idea.

'Never mind,' I said, and jerked free the second time. 'Keep your hands off me, Sheriff. I was trying to do you a favor. Now you know all I know, so I'll be riding.'

I wheeled away and took one step. Hogan grabbed me again and another man grabbed me by the other shoulder. I saw the second man had a star too, so I guessed he was a deputy. Hogan was sore now. I don't know what was going through his head, but he had a kind of animal-like instinct that told him something was wrong with me or I'd have answered the question.

'We ain't got time to wrestle you around,' Hogan said. 'We've got to get moving to stop that gang of lynchers, but you know more about 'em than's good for you. Now I want to know how you found out about all of this.'

'It don't make no never mind, Sheriff,' I said. 'It looks like I'd better have kept on riding. I stopped here to tell you something that I knew was important and I didn't know somebody else had already got the word to you. Now if I've committed a crime, arrest me. Otherwise I'll be riding.'

'Then you ain't fixing to tell me what I want to know?' Hogan demanded.

'No,' I said. 'It ain't important. I've told you what's important.'

Hogan jerked his head at the courthouse. 'Then I'll arrest you and you'll stay in jail till we get back from taking care of these bastards. For all I know you're one of 'em.'

'You've got no cause to hold him, Sheriff,' Jake Herder said. 'I asked him to come and tell you what he knew. I guess that makes me responsible for getting him into trouble. If you've got to arrest somebody, arrest me and let Cassidy ride out of here.'

'Oh, come off of it, Jake,' Hogan said harshly. 'You don't know nothing about this man. He might be a spy or a traitor or who knows what the hell he is. By the time we get back, he'll be ready to answer my question.'

An old man with a white beard shoved his way through the circle of men. 'I've been watching and listening, Abe,' he said, 'and I don't like what's going on here. You have no grounds to arrest this man. If you go ahead, you're opening yourself to legal trouble.'

'You ain't a judge no more, Renfro,' Hogan said, 'so stay out of it. Go on, Jim. Jail him.'

The deputy jammed a gun into my spine. 'Move, mister,' he said.

I moved all right, across the courthouse yard and around the building to the log jail on the back of the lot. He'd pulled my gun when he and Hogan were holding me.

Now he shoved me through the door, followed, and laid my gun on a desk. He opened the cell door, pushed me inside, then shut and locked the door, and left the jail.

I sat down on the bunk and began to curse Hogan and the deputy and the entire town of Jackson and Mule Deer County to boot. I stopped when I ran out of breath and thought about my situation. One fact stood clearly. It was damned hard to do good.

## CHAPTER FIFTEEN

I was hungry. I yelled and banged on the door, but apparently no one else was in the jail. Finally, I lay down on the bunk and stared at the ceiling and wondered how long I'd be here. I'd never been locked up inside a jail. In fact, I had never even been inside a jail, but I'd been here long enough already. When I thought about some men spending months and even years in jail, I wondered why they didn't go loco.

Since I wasn't acquainted with jails, I didn't have any idea whether this one was typical, but either way, this was one hell of a place. It was filthy dirty and smelled of urine and stale sweat and vomit. Maybe it was all some old drunks deserved, and I suspected they were the men who usually got locked up here, but I sure as hell didn't deserve it. The longer I lay there, the madder I got.

It seemed that I'd been there half a day, but I guess it wasn't more than an hour or so when a crippled old man came into the jail office with a plate of food and a cup of coffee. I yelled at him, 'Time you were showing up. I was hungry when they threw me in here.'

'Don't get sassy with me, bud,' the old man said. 'You ain't in no Delmonicos, so be satisfied with what you get.'

'I ain't likely to,' I snapped. 'How long am I gonna be in here?'

'I dunno,' I said. 'It ain't no concern of mine.'

He shoved the plate of food and cup of coffee to me through a slit in the bars beside the door and limped out. I sat down on the bunk and stared at the two fried eggs that stared back at me like a pair of rheumy, orange eyes. The three slices of fat bacon weren't any more attractive, soggy and too much fat and half-cooked. The coffee was black and hot, and was the only part of the meal I could get down without shutting my eyes. I was too hungry to be finicky and I finally ate everything that was on the plate.

I had just finished when the old man with the white beard who had spoken up for me against the sheriff came into the office, took a key off a peg that had been driven into the front wall, and unlocked the cell door.

'I want to visit with you,' he said as he opened the cell door. 'I'm Frank Renfro. I used to be judge here until last election when I decided not to run again.'

'I'm Bruce Cassidy,' I said, and shook hands with him.

Now that I had a good, close look at his face, I decided he wasn't as old as I had thought. It was just that the white hair and beard made him look like a patriarch. I liked him. It was partly because he had taken my part, but it was more than that. He gave me a good, firm handshake, his blue eyes met mine squarely, and he didn't have the slightest trace of the beaten-down appearance that Jake Herder had and which I suspected was true with a good many of the Mule Deer settlers.

Renfro sat down at the desk and motioned for me to sit down in the only other chair in the office. My gun was still on the desk. I picked it up and slid it into my holster. Renfro watched me without saying a word.

'I ain't going back into that filthy hole,' I

107

said.

Renfro nodded. 'I don't blame you. You didn't belong there in the first place.'

'That's right,' I said bitterly. 'I don't figure on ever trying to do a good turn for anybody again as long as I live. It just don't pay.'

He laughed shortly. 'As of right now, I can savvy why you feel that way, but you'll change your mind when you get over your mad. Sit down, Mr. Cassidy. I'd like to know just what happened.'

'Where's my horse?' I demanded. 'All I want to do is to get out of this God-damned town and head back to Oregon. I should have stayed there in the first place.'

'Oh, so you're from Oregon,' he said. 'That's a beautiful state. What part did you live in?'

'Baker County,' I said. 'In the Blue Mountains.'

'Oh yes, I've been through there on the train,' he said. 'Now how did you get involved in Wyoming's troubles?'

If I had walked out right then as I intended to, I'd have saved myself some trouble, but I might have made some for Frank Renfro. I figured Abe Hogan to be a stubborn son of a bitch who never had admitted in his life to having made a mistake. When he got back and found out I was gone, he'd raise hell and prop it up with a chunk.

I sat down and told Renfro the whole story,

beginning with my father's trouble and my killing Smiley Rehn, then about Chauncey Dunn showing up and hiring me, and how I'd joined the invaders and killed Hank Gibson. The part that really interested him, of course, was the shooting of Peewee Curry and the fact that I had seen it done.

When I finished, he said, 'I had guessed part of it, but I wanted to hear the whole story.'

'What's going to happen to the invaders?' I asked. 'I don't feel quite the way I did when I left Oregon. I don't really want to see all of them swinging from cottonwood limbs.'

'Funny how a man's attitude changes when he actually sees a thing happen and gets to know the people who are involved,' he said. 'Take your Dr. Orr. I don't know the man. I've never heard of him that I know of, but I can savvy how he could have been persuaded to join the outfit and then discovered he didn't have the stomach for it. It takes a certain kind of lowdown blackguard to shoot down a man the way Curry was shot down.'

'Sure, I can savvy how Orr felt,' I said, 'but he didn't want me to leave and warn the settlers. He wanted the invaders to finish the job they came for, even though he didn't have the guts to help them finish.'

Renfro shrugged. 'Some men are like that. It was to his interest, he thought, for the invaders to succeed in doing what they set out to do, so he wanted them to be successful regardless of his personal feelings.' He tapped his fingers on the desk, studying me, then he said, 'Mr. Cassidy, I believe in the law. It's a passion with me. I am absolutely convinced that the only way we can be governed in a great country like this is by making our laws work.'

He leaned forward. 'I admit I feel this way because I am a lawyer and I have been a judge for many years, but I've seen too many cases of individuals or groups of people who take the law into their own hands. It invariably results in tragedy. The law may not operate with complete justice at all times, but if it doesn't, it is usually because of the dishonesty or lack of ability of the men who enforce it.

'This is where the invaders are wrong. They certainly have a case. As much as I like my friends and neighbors, I have to admit they have done wrong in stealing cattle from the big cowmen, but there are ways of using the law to protect them which they have refused to try.

'They are the kind of men who are used to having their own way, so they come in here with an armed force expecting to have it again. Regardless of what crimes Dawson and Curry have done, killing them was murder and they can't make anything else out of it.'

He reached into his pocket and took out a cigar, bit off the end and lit it. He chewed on it for a moment, then went on, 'I'm afraid that our people may make the same mistake. If they capture and hang these men, that will be murder, too. I think you came to that conclusion when you said you didn't want to see these men swinging from cottonwood limbs.'

'That's right,' I said. 'I don't have any great liking for Yancey and Dunn and Walters, but I've had a change of thinking. It's, well, it's a . . .'

I stopped, not finding the right words. Renfro finished my sentence for me. 'It's a matter of two wrongs not making a right.'

I nodded. 'That's about it.'

'But you do want to see justice done?'

I hesitated. I had never met anyone like this Frank Renfro. I was convinced he was an honest, decent man who wanted what was best for the people of Mule Deer County, but I also sensed he was an idealist and not the most practical of men. He could talk all he wanted to about law, but I knew there was nothing my mother and I could have done for my father when Gibson and Rehn took his manhood from him. Too, I could have asked him what the big cowmen could have done to protect themselves and still stay within the law. The settlers had their men in office who would enforce the law to their advantage just as the cowmen had done when they had their men in office.

I saw no point of pushing at him. In principle I agreed with him, so finally I said,

'Sure, I want to see justice done, but I want to get out of here. I've had enough of Mule Deer County's jail and Abe Hogan's brand of justice.'

'Oh, I understand that,' he said quickly, 'but please don't leave until you have done your part in bringing justice about. I want you to come and live at my house for the time being. I'll see that you get paid for your time. My wife's a good cook.'

He pointed a forefinger at me. 'Maybe you haven't thought about it, but you are the one man who can convict the invaders. Now there's bound to be a fight. There's nothing you or I can do about that. Hogan and some of his men, the hot heads, may get carried away and murder the invaders. I couldn't stop it if I were there. I'm hoping it won't be that way. I'm hoping that Hogan will remember that he is an officer of the law and that he will take them prisoners and bring them in to stand trial.'

'I don't see where I . . .'

'There will be a trial,' he interrupted. 'If we permit the law to do the job, and you testify to what you saw, any jury will convict these men for the murder of Peewee Curry. You are the one witness who can do this.'

I sat there a moment thinking about what Renfro had said. He was probably right, but I didn't want to stay here. Being the main witness at a big trial like that would be didn't appeal to me, either. Something else did.

Maybe it was my crazy sense of humor, but I wanted to see what Abe Hogan would do when he got back and found I wasn't in jail. More than that, I wanted to see his face when Renfro told him I was the key man when it came to convicting the invaders.

Hogan wasn't that important really. Oh, I had reason to hate him and I wanted to see him get his comeuppance. I still sympathized with the settlers and I wanted to see the invaders punished. I believed in law and justice just as Renfro did, although I would never say it was a passion with me. I wasn't logical and I knew it, but it was my personal feeling about Abe Hogan that made up my mind.

'All right,' I said. 'I'll do it.'

'Good.' Renfro rose. 'Let's go sample my wife's cooking and you can tell me whether I'm a liar or not.'

## CHAPTER SIXTEEN

Frank Renfro's house was a two-story frame building across the creek from the courthouse and business block. This was the main residential section of town, the trees shaded by fair-sized cottonwoods. Many of the houses had white picket fences in front of them, but Renfro's fence was iron, a definite mark of distinction. Too, most of the houses had boardwalks along the front of their yards. Jackson was not an old town, but somehow it gave the appearance of age, stability and permanence.

He opened the gate for me and stepped back for me to go ahead. The yard was well cared for, and although it was still early in the year, a few flowers were in bloom close to the house. Daffodils, mostly, I saw, and guessed there would be more flowers when the warm weather came. Two lilac bushes were on opposite sides of the path that led to the porch, but it would be some time before they bloomed.

The front door had one large pane of clear glass that was surrounded by small pieces of colored glass. Renfro opened the door, and again stepped back for me to enter the house. I did, and he followed, closing the door behind him.

I smelled food cooking, a good smell. You can tell almost as much from the smell of food as you can from the taste, and this was one hell of a good smell after having that stinking jail breakfast.

'Lucinda,' Renfro called. 'Mr. Cassidy is here.'

His wife came into the living room from the kitchen, wiping her hands on her apron. She was a tall woman, almost as tall as Renfro, spare, with gray hair that was pulled back severely from her forehead. I had the impression that she would have fitted back in old New England, and that she was a matriarch who was a fitting wife for patriarchal Frank Renfro.

She extended a bony hand to me. 'I'm pleased to meet you, Mr. Cassidy. I take it you will be staying with us or you wouldn't be here.'

'I guess that's right,' I said. 'You know, your husband said you were a good cook and from what I smell, I'd guess he was dead right.'

She permitted herself a small smile, then she said, 'I'll let you be the judge of that, Mr. Cassidy. Sit down and make yourself to home.'

I sat down in the black leather chair. Renfro moved across the room and stood with his back to a huge stone fireplace that had the tallest brass andirons I had ever seen. I glanced around the room. The furniture was good, certainly above average in a town as far from the railroad as Jackson was, and where people, by necessity, were forced to pay the cost of freighting everything in by wagon.

The floor was nearly covered by a very large rag rug. There were several rockers, a heavy black couch that matched the chair where I sat, and a walnut, claw-footed stand in the middle of the room. A lamp with an ornate shade was on the stand.

On the far wall was a large bookcase filled with what I later found to be classics such as the *Odyssey*, Plutarch's *Lives*, and

Shakespeare's plays.

A framed motto hung above the fireplace, the words HOME SWEET HOME embroidered on it in red thread. Nowhere in the room was there the slightest hint of disorder or a speck of dust. Not that I was critical of a woman's housekeeping. It was just that the perfection of the room made me uneasy. Nothing, absolutely nothing, was out of place.

The appearance of the room was that of an elegance a notch higher than that of the average family and certainly better than anything I had ever seen. Frank Renfro was a fairly wealthy man, I judged, and probably still had a comfortable law practice. I wondered if he would be risking all of this by taking me into his house. The thought vaguely upset me.

He lit up another cigar, amused eyes on me. He asked, 'You approve?'

I nodded. 'It's a fine room, Mr. Renfro. I expect it's the best in Jackson.'

'Well, one of the best,' he said. 'I hope you will find it comfortable.'

'I'm sure I will,' I said, and yet I still had that uneasy feeling, that maybe I had tracked in a speck of dust.

A moment later Mrs. Renfro called us into the dining room. The cherrywood table was covered by a white lace cloth. The dishes were fancy, blue with a scene of a team and carriage on the plates. The eating tools were silver. She

116

said the dishes were Wedgwood, whatever that was. A massive sideboard also of cherrywood that was filled with dishes was set against one wall.

I don't remember exactly what was in that first meal. I was too much aware of the luxury that surrounded me. I'd have enjoyed the meal more if we'd been eating in the kitchen off a table covered by oil cloth, but I know it was a good meal and that I ate an enormous amount of food. It was the first real meal I'd had for a long time.

When we finished and rose from the table, I thanked Mrs. Renfro and told her it was indeed a good meal. She said, 'Thank you, Mr. Cassidy. I'll expect you for supper. I like to cook and I enjoy seeing men eat.'

As we turned toward the living room, Renfro said, 'I'll show you your room upstairs so you'll know where you'll be sleeping. I suppose the next few days will hang heavy on your hands, you being a man of action like you are.'

'I ain't used to sitting in a house,' I admitted, 'or even loafing around town.'

'You might explore the town,' he said. 'Have a drink or two and maybe find someone to visit with, though practically every able-minded man in town left with Hogan.'

'Mr. Cassidy,' Mrs. Renfro said, 'your clothes are filthy. If you will go downtown and buy yourself new clothes, I'll wash the ones you are wearing. When you get back, I'll have some hot water and you can take a bath. We have a tub in a small room behind the kitchen.'

That took me back a little. I'd never had a woman tell me before that I needed a bath and a change of clothes, but I knew she was right. I said, 'I guess I'm pretty gamey, all right.'

'You are,' she said. 'You will also find a razor, soap, a brush, and a mirror in the bathroom.'

Well, there was nothing shy or backward about Mrs. Renfro. I did what she said, and by the middle of the afternoon I looked and felt like a different man and I sure as hell smelled better. I spent the rest of the day tramping around town and up and down the creek, and wondered how I was going to get through the next week or more without anything to do.

As it turned out, I didn't have as much trouble as I thought I would have. I had a drink or two in the Red Front saloon and gabbed with the bartender, an old man who had come into the country before there was a Jackson and had seen a lot of changes, most of which he didn't like a little bit.

Either through one of the Renfros or the bartender, the story got out that I was going to testify against the invaders for Peewee Curry's murder. I'd told the bartender, and I'd guess he was the one who spread the story because I judged the Renfros to be close-mouthed people.

Anyhow, folks, mostly women, began stopping me on the street and introducing themselves and telling me they appreciated what I was going to do and it was high time that law and order came to Mule Deer County. None of them asked me how I happened to see the shooting or why I was with the invaders, a good deal different attitude than Abe Hogan had had.

I saddled up my horse and took some long rides back into the foothills of the Big Horns. I read a little bit, though I didn't find much in the Renfro library that was to my liking. I usually spent the evenings talking to Judge Renfro.

Sometimes Mrs. Renfro would come into the living room and sit down and spend the evening embroidering. She seldom said anything, but when she did, Frank gave her absolute attention as if every statement she made was a profound one. She was, to me, a most remarkable woman, but one who would be hell to live with.

I kept watch for someone to show up who would know what had happened between Hogan's group and the invaders, but we heard nothing for several days. Then one afternoon a man rode in with the story.

What had happened was incredible to me and even more incredible to the Judge. The invaders got as far north as Arrowhead when they ran into Hogan's bunch. They holed up in the Arrowhead buildings and found they were outnumbered. The settlers surrounded them but couldn't root them out without losing a lot of men. On the other hand, the invaders were nailed down and couldn't get away.

Hogan decided to hang tight and starve the invaders into surrendering which is exactly what would have happened eventually, but before it reached that point, two troops of cavalry came galloping onto the scene with bugles blowing and flags waving.

'You'd have thought they were saving us from the Sioux,' the man said in disgust, 'but they sure as hell did save the God-damned lynchers. We'd have given 'em a taste of their own ropes if the army hadn't horned in.'

Later we learned that on the first night of the siege the invaders got a man through the settler lines. He rode until he came to a telegraph station and sent a message to the governor. The governor wired the Wyoming senators in Washington. The senators got the president out of bed, told him what had happened, and he ordered the troops from the fort nearest Jackson to go to the rescue.

'You can depend on one thing,' Renfro said angrily. 'If the shoe had been on the other foot, the damned governor would never have turned a hair. It just goes to prove that you'd better be on the right side when you yell for help.'

'Now what?' I said. 'Looks to me like I

might as well start riding.'

'No, no, no,' Renfro shouted. 'By God, no. We'll try them and we'll convict them and then we'll hang them.'

'How do you figure to get them away from the army post?' I asked.

'We'll do it,' he said. 'I don't know how, but we will. We've still got some law and order around here.'

I wasn't so sure of that, but I figured I'd know more about Mule Deer County law when Abe Hogan got back to town. He did, two days later.

## CHAPTER SEVENTEEN

Most of Hogan's men spent some time in town after the army took over. I did not see either Jake Herder or Jinglebob Turner. Apparently they went directly home when the fight was over. Most of the men were settlers who stopped for a drink. The rest were townsmen who were glad to get back to their places of business.

I spent most of those two days downtown listening to what the men had to say. A lot of powder was burned apparently, but no one was killed, though a couple of the invaders were hard hit and might die. Three of the settlers got tagged, but they had minor wounds.

The main thing, and it seemed to be true of every man I heard, was that they were mad. The grub that the invaders had brought with them never got to Arrowhead. The settlers cut the wagon off and turned it around and ordered the cook to head back to Casper. Of course there was a limited supply of food at Arrowhead, and all of the settlers I talked to insisted that it wouldn't have been long until they would have starved the invaders out and they would have surrendered. Now they'd get off scot-free to do it all over again.

I asked several men what they would have done if the invaders had surrendered. To a man they said, 'Why, we would have strung 'em up.'

'Without a trial?' I asked.

'Oh, we'd have tried 'em,' one said, 'and then we would have watched 'em swing. They wouldn't have been in no shape to ever hit us again.'

Another man said disdainfully, 'Trial? Hell, they were guilty or they would never have been here. What do you think they came for?'

The others just turned and walked off. The story that I was going to testify was repeated to all of them sooner or later, and when they heard that, they would say, 'If you saw Carry killed, you know what they would have done to the rest of us and you know what they've got coming.' Eventually they'd get around to asking, 'What were you doing with 'em?'

I couldn't answer that truthfully, knowing they wouldn't understand, so I dodged the question by saying I just happened to be there. If they pressed me, I'd say I was looking for work. I figured that if I told the truth, they'd hang me on general principles, particularly since they had been frustrated by the army.

Sooner or later the talk always got around to what would have happened if Hogan had not been warned and sent the word out to the settlers. 'They'd have strung up every man on their list and gone on home and nobody would have touched 'em,' one man said.

'You can bet your bottom dollar that if it had been the other way around,' another man said bitterly, 'the governor would never have wired the senators and the senators would never have gone to the president and the president would never have called the army out.'

I could understand the bitterness and I didn't doubt that they would have lynched the invaders if they'd got their hands on them, and there would have been hell to pay if they had. Well, it hadn't happened, and I had a hunch that Walters and his men would walk out of the army post free men, which was what a good many of the settlers were saying. I didn't say that to Renfro, though. He was determined they'd be tried and convicted. He was a big man in Mule Deer County, but I didn't figure he was that big in the state of Wyoming.

When I got back to Renfro's house the evening of the second day, the Judge said, 'Cassidy, I want you to stay here in the house from now on. Sooner or later the real story of how you happened to be there to see Curry shot is going to get out and the boys won't savvy. They'll figure you got boogery and ran out like Doc Orr did.'

I nodded. 'I've been thinking the same thing, but I don't know that I'm going to stay inside your house for the next six months.'

'Oh, it won't be that long,' he said. 'We'll get the trial started as soon as we can, maybe in a month or less.'

I didn't believe it, knowing that power and money were on the side of the invaders, but I didn't argue. I'd do what Renfro said even if I got cabin fever because I'd had the same notion and it was enough to make me a little jumpy. I figured it was going to be worse when Hogan showed up and found out I wasn't in jail. I was standing by a window in the front room thinking about him when I saw him ride by.

'There's the sheriff, Judge,' I said. 'I figure we'll be hearing from him before long.'

'We sure will,' Renfro said. 'I hope you can control your temper. If you shoot him, every man who was down there at Arrowhead will come after you and I won't be able to save your neck. The trouble is I feel responsible for it.'

'You can count on one thing,' I said. 'He's not putting me back in that jail. I'll kill him first.'

'Then we'd better figure out a way to handle this,' he said. 'It's going to be touch and go. I know Abe. He's honest, but as you've found out, he's a bullhead.'

'Is his deputy back yet?'

Renfro shook his head. 'I don't think so. It's a good thing he isn't because he'd back Abe through hell and high water, and that'd just make Abe worse.' He stood beside me at the window for a time stroking his beard, his forehead furrowed with thought. Then he said, 'I'd better go see Abe. Maybe I can talk some sense into him.'

He took his hat down from the antlers near the door and left the house. It wasn't long until he was back. He said, 'It didn't take Abe long to find out where you're staying. The next five minutes are going to decide a lot of things, Cassidy. Just don't jump the gun.'

I'd told him enough times how I felt, so I didn't repeat it. I eased my gun in the holster and watched Hogan as he reined up in front of the house and came striding up the path, his big tough face set in hard lines. He hit the porch, his boot heels cracking sharply on the boards, and made it to the door in two long steps. He yanked savagely at the bell pull, almost jerking it out of the wall.

Renfro opened the door. Hogan didn't wait

for him to ask him to come into the house. He simply charged past the Judge and faced me. I stood about fifteen feet from him, my gun in my hand. He bawled, 'I left you in jail. How'd you get out?'

'I let him out,' Renfro said. 'I've kept him here ever since. Sit down, Abe. I want to talk to you.'

'I've got no time to talk,' Hogan said. 'I'm taking this bastard back to jail.'

'I don't think so,' I said. 'I spent a few hours in your stinking jail, bastard. I ain't going back.'

'Don't call me bastard,' Hogan bellowed. 'By God, I'll show you who gives the orders in this town.'

I motioned with my gun. 'Show me,' I said.

He looked at my face and then at the gun, and raised his gaze back to my face. For the moment he seemed uncertain about what he should do. I said, 'Hogan, I'll call any man a bastard who throws me into jail without a charge of any kind. If you try putting me back in there, I'll kill you.'

He took a long breath, his gaze still pinned on my face. I guess he believed me. He wheeled to face Renfro. He said, 'Judge, you're the man I ought to jail. Where did you get the authority to release this man?'

'I took the authority because we need him. He's right about you not having anything to charge him with. He came here to warn you just like he said.'

Hogan threw up his hands. 'Bullshit! Don't you know who he is? Dunn hired him in Oregon to come here and join up with the invaders. He's as bad as any of 'em, worse maybe because he got scared and pulled out. That's why he came here claiming he was aiming to warn us. He's gonna go to the fort and live with the rest of them murdering sons of bitches.'

'They'll kill him,' Renfro said.

'That's what I'm hoping for,' Hogan said grimly.

Renfro shook his head. 'You're hopeless, Abe. I'm thinking about this case when it comes to the trial. Do you think you'll get any of the men who are at the fort to testify against themselves?'

'Hell no.'

'Just remember that they didn't break any law by riding into Mule Deer County,' Renfro went on. 'They didn't commit any crime that we can hold them for until they actually murdered Peewee Curry.'

'But hell, Judge,' Hogan exploded, 'we all know why they came. They even had a list of marked men they were going to murder.'

'Do you have that list?'

'No, but.'

'You think it still exists?'

'Probably not, but . . .'

'Do you think you can even prove it ever

127

existed?'

'No, I reckon not.'

'All right, now you listen to me and you listen good. Cassidy did not take part in the shooting. He was ordered by Major Walters to attend to the horses. You probably have heard that from talking to Walters and Yancey and the others.'

Hogan moistened his lips with the tip of his tongue. He shot a glance at me, then looked at the Judge again. 'Yeah, as a matter of fact, I did.'

'Maybe Doc Orr would testify to the same thing because he was with Cassidy,' Renfro went on, 'but we don't have Orr, we don't know where he is, and the chances are he's clean out of the state by now. We do have Cassidy and he's agreed to testify to what he saw when Curry was shot. Without him we don't have a case that's fool proof. We might make it stick in Mule Deer County, but we probably won't have the trial here. Nobody else saw the shooting who can testify without incriminating himself, but you keep saying you hope they kill Cassidy when you take him to the fort.'

Hogan finally saw the light. He walked across the room and back, his hands jammed into his pockets. He shook his head, glowering at me. He said in a surly voice, 'It gravels the hell out of me to think you might be of some use to us, but I reckon you will be. There's one

128

thing you'd better understand. If you don't testify like you said or if you try to get out of the county, I will throw you back into jail and I'll lose the key.'

'Now there's one thing you'd better know.' I was just about as mad as Hogan was and I was getting damned tired of listening to his threats. 'You keep pushing at me and telling me what you're going to do to me and I won't testify.'

'All right, Abe,' Renfro said patiently. 'I'll take care of Cassidy, so quit warning him about jail. The only thing that worries me is that the invaders probably know by now that he's here and they know as well as we do what he can do to them. I think there's a good chance they'll try to murder him. I'll need your help to keep him alive.'

Hogan shook his head. 'Naw, they ain't that smart.' He walked to the door, turned and scowled at me for a full minute, then he wheeled and left the house.

'What's the matter with him?' I asked. 'He acts like he resents me doing anything for the settlers. He hates me like poison and he's got no reason for it.'

'No reason,' Renfro agreed, 'except that he made up his mind when you first showed up with Jake Herder that you were on the other side. He always has a lot of trouble changing his mind once it gets made up. He just can't see you in any other light.'

I stood there by the window thinking about

the sheriff. I'd met up with some stubborn men in my time, but Abe Hogan was the prize.

## CHAPTER EIGHTEEN

The sun was almost down and the light had become thin. I heard Mrs. Renfro in the kitchen preparing supper. The smell was tantalizing. She had been to some kind of church meeting and was late with supper. The Judge had gone back into his study so I was alone in the living room.

Suddenly I had a feeling that a man was watching me from the vacant lot across the street. There was a ditch along the far edge of the street which supported an ugly growth of weeds. The lot was covered by equally large weeds tall enough and thick enough to hide a man.

Actually I couldn't see him, but I was certain he was there. Maybe it was that crazy feeling you get when you know someone is watching you but you can't see him physically. Or maybe I had caught a stray glint of sunlight on a rifle barrel or just a slight movement of the weeds.

To this day I don't know for sure why I did what I did, but I had lived with danger a good deal of my life and I suppose a man develops some kind of a weird sixth sense that gives him a warning at the crucial moment.

Anyhow, Mrs. Renfro came into the room from the kitchen just then, calling, 'Supper's ready, Mr. Cassidy, Frank, time to wash up.'

I wheeled from the window, saw that she was directly in line with me and the man in the weeds. I grabbed her and without saying a word, dragged her to the floor. She screamed and kicked, then stopped abruptly because in that same instant a rifle cracked and I heard the tingling of glass on the floor. Mrs. Renfro cried, 'Is somebody trying to kill me?'

The Judge ran into the room, demanding, 'What happened?'

'Stay down,' I said to Mrs. Renfro, and wormed my way across the floor into the kitchen.

I was on my feet the second I was out of sight of the man on the other side of the street. I raced across the kitchen and the back porch, then hugged the side of the house to the front corner. I had my gun in my hand as I peered around the corner trying not to expose myself. I still couldn't see anyone, but I noticed that the tops of the weeds were waving about twenty feet on the other side of the ditch, so I cut loose with my Colt.

I laid four shots in close to the ground a foot or two apart, then with one shell left in my gun, I sprinted across the street. Maybe it was stupid. If the dry gulcher had stayed where he had been, he could have cut me down with one shot, but I figured he was pulling out. If I didn't get him then, I wouldn't get him at all, and he'd be alive to try again.

He must have heard me coming because he apparently panicked before I was across the street. He jumped up into view and tried to bring his rifle up, but he never got the barrel quite leveled. My slug caught him in the chest and he pulled the trigger, a convulsive jerk that sent a bullet five feet over my head. He went back down into the weeds, and by the time I reached him, he was dead.

I turned and waved to the house, then stood staring down at the man. I'd never seen him before and I certainly had never done anything to hurt him or make him hate me enough to try to kill me. He was middle age, poorly dressed, with a scar down one side of his cheek, a nondescript-looking man who might have been riding the grub line. As soon as Renfro reached me, he swore in surprise.

'It's Dud Loomis,' Renfro said. 'I've seen him around town lots of times. Never works much, but I understand he hangs around the fort and does odd jobs.'

Renfro knelt beside him and went through his pockets. The man had the usual track: a knife, a handful of change, an elk tooth, and a corkscrew. Renfro must have felt his money belt because he opened up the man's shirt and trousers and pulled the belt free. He whistled when he opened it.

132

'My God, Cassidy,' Renfro said, 'there must be five hundred dollars here. I never knew him to have more than ten or fifteen at any one time. I'll bet this is the most money he ever had in his entire life.'

A crowd began gathering around us that included Abe Hogan. He demanded, 'What happened?'

'I killed a man, Sheriff,' I said. 'Are you going to hold me?'

'That's a crazy question, Cassidy,' Renfro said angrily. 'Of course he's not going to hold you.' He turned to Hogan. 'He saved my wife's life, Abe. I guess he saw Loomis over here in the weeds.' He handed the money belt to Hogan. 'You'd better take care of this. I just pulled it off Loomis.'

Hogan took the belt, hefted it, and looked inside. 'Now how did that old bastard get hold of this much dinero?'

'What would be your guess?' Renfro asked.

'Maybe held up a bank or a stage,' Hogan answered. 'All I know about him is that he worked around the fort just enough to eat and buy a few drinks.'

'Did you see him when you were over there today?' Renfro asked.

Hogan scratched his cheek. 'Yeah, I seen him. It was a kind of funny thing. I'd been quizzing some of the prisoners and when I left, I remember he was talking to Major Walters. I couldn't see why a no-good like Loomis would have anything to talk about to Walters, but . . .'

He stopped and stared blankly at me. Renfro nodded. 'I guess you've got the same notion I have. I told you they'd make a try at Cassidy.'

'I still don't know what happened just now,' Hogan said.

I told him, adding, 'I took a chance charging across the street, but I don't like to be shot at and I was afraid he'd get away.'

Hogan motioned to a couple of men standing beside him. 'Lug the carcass over to the coroner's office.' He turned to me. 'No, I ain't gonna hold you, Cassidy. I'd call it justifiable homicide.' He nodded at Renfro. 'I want to talk to Cassidy. Let's go inside.'

'Of course,' Renfro said, and led the way across the street to his house.

I went in first, then Hogan, and Renfro came in last and shut the door. Mrs. Renfro was sitting in the big leather chair. She'd been crying and she still looked very upset. She said, 'Mr. Cassidy, I kicked you and I screamed at you, and I apologize. I just didn't know what you were doing or why you were doing it.'

'It's all right, Mrs. Renfro,' I said. 'I never would have forgiven myself if my presence in your house had caused your death.'

'Well, it didn't,' she said, 'and I thank you for what you did. Now I'll go finish putting supper on the table. You'll stay and eat with us, Mr. Hogan?'

'I'd like to,' he said, 'but I've got to get back to the courthouse.'

Hogan turned to me and grinned. It was the first time I had seen the slightest hint of good humor on his face and I was surprised to see it then. 'Well, Cassidy,' he said, 'if that bunch of murdering bastards think you're important enough to dry gulch, I guess you're important enough for us to take care of. I ain't figuring on jailing you, but the jail might be the safest place for you.'

'No,' I said. 'I'd rather have them fill me full of lead than to live in your jail. I know I can't stay here, but I'll find some place.'

Hogan was visibly troubled. He turned to Renfro. 'You got any idea, Judge?'

'I'll hide him out,' Renfro said. 'Don't worry about it, Abe. I'll take care of it.'

But now that Hogan had shifted position, he was just as stubborn as he had been on the other side. He shook his head. 'No, I ain't gonna leave it up to you. I want to know what you're fixing to do. Now that we've got him alive, I aim to keep him that way.'

Renfro laughed. 'I reckon you're admitting you've been making a mistake about Cassidy.'

Hogan grinned again. 'Well now, Judge, you've never heard me say out loud that I made a mistake. I just want to know what you're fixing to do.'

'I'll take him back into the mountains tonight while it's dark,' Renfro said. 'That way

135

nobody in town will see us go or know the direction we're taking. We'll have to see that he gets supplies every two or three weeks. Tonight we'll take a pack horse so he'll have enough grub to last a month.'

Hogan shook his head, his face hardening. 'It won't do, Judge. You can't just take him up some canyon and dump him.'

I guess he figured I'd keep on riding and I just might do it, I thought. I'd had enough of the whole business. When it comes to getting dry gulched, I figure it had better be about something I had a stake in and I sure didn't have a stake in this deal any longer.

Renfro got the point, all right, but he didn't put it into words and neither did I. The Judge said, 'All right, damn it, I'll tell you. I'm going to take him up to old man Fanchon's place. He'll look out for Cassidy. He owes me that and then some.'

'Fanchon!' Hogan blurted. 'My God, Judge, them Fanchon kids will kill him. They're the meanest bastards I ever ran into.'

Renfro shrugged. 'Or he'll kill them. Oh, I think the old man can handle them. I figure the county can afford to pay him something for looking after Cassidy.'

Suddenly Hogan laughed, a good, warm sound that I didn't think he was capable of making. 'All right, Judge, I guess old man Fanchon can keep him safe and sound.' He turned to me. 'There's a good-looking girl up

136

there, but don't get any ideas. She's a woods colt. You won't get nowhere with her. All right, I guess your supper's about ready. We'll let you know when the trial comes up, Cassidy.'

I nodded and didn't say anything until he left. Then I said, 'Judge, you better tell me something about this outfit before I go up there. It didn't sound good to me.'

'Oh, you'll like them, all right,' Renfro said. 'It's always a challenge to be around the Fanchon boys. They're twins, twenty years old, and they're just as mean as Hogan said they were. I figure you can take care of yourself with them, but I'm not so sure about the girl.'

I'd decided I'd go along since I couldn't stay here. I'd come this far. I might as well go the rest of the way, though it was strange how my feelings had changed about the big cowmen. I guess Renfro had taught me something about the necessity for the law handling a situation like this.

Anyhow, I didn't think one old man and two twenty-year-old kids could hold me if I decided to ride on. Besides, there was a girl. It might be an interesting experience.

## CHAPTER NINETEEN

As soon as we finished supper, Renfro took me down a flight of stairs into their cellar. He

137

said, 'The stores aren't open now, so we'll get your first supplies here. After that I'll buy them in a store and charge them to the county. There's a good trout stream that runs past your cabin and chances are you'll shoot a deer or two, but I'll bring you most of your supplies.'

Renfro had enough food in his cellar to last all winter. He filled a couple of sacks with bacon, ham, coffee, sugar, flour, and a variety of canned goods. He straightened up and looked at the shelves and then at me.

'See anything else you want?' he asked.

'No,' I said, 'except that I'll need ammunition for both my Winchester and my forty-five.'

'We'll get it upstairs,' he said.

'Why have you got so much grub stored away?' I asked.

'Habit mostly, I guess,' he said. 'Lucinda insists on buying stuff as fast as we use it up, so we keep about a year's supply on hand along with the beefsteak we buy and what she raises in her garden. When we first settled here, the town got snowed in all winter so it was every man for himself. We had a store, but by the end of January there wasn't enough left on the shelves to feed a sparrow, so we saw to it that we always had plenty right here at home.

He picked up one sack and went upstairs. I followed with the other. He said over his shoulder, 'Funny how habit regulates a man. I guess we'd all have a hell of a time just living if we didn't have a set of habits to keep us going.'

We set the sacks down in the kitchen beside the back door. Mrs. Renfro was washing dishes. She looked up, her gaze on me for a moment, then on her husband. She said, 'Frank, I don't like this. I'd rather have Mr. Cassidy stay here. The Fanchons are an evil family and you know it.'

'Now, now Lucinda,' Renfro said. 'It's for your and my safety as much as his that he's leaving. I know the Fanchons aren't the best human beings in the world, but Cassidy will get along. If I'm sizing him up right, he'll manage just about anywhere.'

He jerked his head at me and I followed him into his study. I had not been in the room before and the number of law books that occupied one wall amazed me. A desk and two chairs were the only pieces of furniture in the room.

'I didn't know there were so many law books in the world,' I said.

He laughed. 'I don't use many of them. I've spent a lifetime gathering them. Lucinda says I'm crazy and that I keep myself broke buying books I never use and I reckon she's right, being near the end of my legal career.'

Renfro shook his head. 'I don't know, Cassidy. Maybe I've wasted my time in this county. Sometimes I think it never will grow up, but I love it and I love the people, and I'm

139

God-damned tired of having a few big cowmen run the state the way they've been doing.'

He opened a desk drawer and took out two boxes of .30-.30 shells and two more for my .45. 'That enough?' he asked.

'It ought to be,' I said. 'I don't expect to get into a war.'

'You never know what to expect when you're with the Fanchons,' he said, 'but I don't think you'll have any trouble with them.'

'The more I hear about the Fanchons,' I said, 'the more I wonder why you're taking me to 'em.'

He laughed. 'I guess it's enough to make a man wonder. I'll say one thing. You'll never meet another family like them. As a matter of fact, I wouldn't take you up there except that it's the best place to go. No dry gulchers will find you without the Fanchons knowing about it. The old man owes me considerable, which same he knows. I've kept him out of the pen more than once. It's the boys who are dangerous, but the old man keeps them in line. I don't know much about the girl except that she's a pretty little thing.'

He picked up the boxes of ammunition and, returning to the kitchen, dropped them into the sacks. He said, 'My saddle horse and pack animal are in my barn. I'll saddle up while you go to Barney Schrock's livery stable and get your horse. Wait for me at the north end of Main Street. Don't say anything to Barney about where we're going or why.'

I nodded and turned to Mrs. Renfro. 'Thank you for your trouble,' I said. 'You're the best cook I ever ran into.'

She wiped her hands on her apron and crossed the kitchen to me. 'You take care of yourself, Mr. Cassidy. If we never see each other again, I hope you'll always think kindly of me.'

She kissed me on the cheek and turned away quickly and began wiping her eyes. I didn't know what to say. I was surprised and a little embarrassed, so I left the house without saying anything else. I thought how wrong I'd been about her. When I had first seen her I had judged her to be a stern, cold woman who would have fitted into the Puritan life of colonial days, but I'd been wrong. She was a very warm person who had enjoyed having me in her home. I would indeed think kindly of her just as I would the Judge.

I didn't have any trouble getting my horse, although I was afraid I would, thinking that Hogan might have ordered Schrock to keep the animal in the stable, but maybe he had passed the word to release him after the attempt had been made on my life.

Anyhow, I paid my bill and rode out through the archway into the street without the liveryman asking why I wasn't staying to testify at the trial. When the thought occurred to me that Hogan might have told the liveryman where I was going, I didn't like that notion a little bit.

I waited at the edge of town for about ten minutes before Renfro showed up leading his pack horse. He asked, 'Any trouble?'

'No,' I said. 'Should I have had trouble?'

'I didn't think you would,' he said, 'but I didn't know how Hogan had left your horse. He might have told Schrock not to release him without a written order. If that had been the case, we would have had to go to Hogan for such an order. I guess he made up his mind to let you go.'

'I thought he had the way he talked this evening,' I said.

'He's got an ornery way of changing his mind,' Renfro said, 'but as long as he didn't, we're all right.'

We struck out, heading north on the main road for about a mile, then we swung west toward the Big Horns. There was a full moon and the sky was clear, so we had no trouble following the narrow dirt road. Presently the foothills closed in on us and we were in a canyon with a fair-sized creek to our right.

By the time we had ridden two hours the canyon had narrowed, the walls very steep, and now the moon was not even visible. The light had thinned so much that we couldn't see where we were going most of the time.

'We're far enough from town so it's not likely anyone will be along,' Renfro said. 'Not much travel on this road. It doesn't go over the top and not many people live up here. I guess the Fanchons are the last ones. We might as well camp and ride by daylight. The Fanchons don't like for anyone to come up on them after dark anyway.'

I guess Renfro knew where we were because we reined off into a side canyon, stopping about fifty yards from the main stream. We built a small fire because the night had turned cold, as it did at this altitude even in the summer.

We offsaddled and staked out the horses, then sat by the fire for a time. Neither of us felt like talking. I had a hunch Renfro was having second thoughts about taking me to the Fanchons. I had a few myself, although it sounded like an adventure and I'll admit I was curious after what I had heard about the Fanchons.

Presently Renfro yawned. 'I guess I'll roll in, Cassidy,' he said. 'It'll be a long day tomorrow by the time I get back home.'

I lay with my head on my saddle, the blanket over me, and stared at the dark sky through the limbs of a nearby pine tree. I heard the faint whisper of the little creek that ran past our camp, the creaking of the trees as the wind rushed down the canyon, and presently a coyote lifted his voice in a mournful call from some distant rim.

This was the kind of situation I loved,

mountains and solitude and the company of a friend. I had not known Frank Renfro long, but I considered him a very good friend and I had learned to respect him as I did few men.

He had spoken up for me that first day I was in Jackson when Hogan jailed me, he had got me out of jail and had given me a place to live, and now he was taking me to a place where he thought I would be safe. I had a hunch I wouldn't, but it was only a hunch and that was not enough reason to speak to Renfro about it.

He struck me as being one of the few unselfish men I had ever met. He had strong ideals about law and order, and I suspected he was one of the men, maybe the only man, in Mule Deer County that Abe Hogan was afraid to buck.

At times I regretted ever signing on with Chauncey Dunn. It certainly had not worked out the way I had hoped or expected. Now, thinking about what had happened since I had left the K Bar, I discovered I had no regrets. I had learned a good deal in a short space of time from Frank Renfro. From Mrs. Renfro, too. At least they were two good human beings, and in my experience, they were rare.

Renfro woke at dawn and I rustled some wood and built a fire while he took care of the horses. He was a tireless and energetic man for his age. I had a feeling he knew these mountains as well as any man.

We ate breakfast and struck out again, the

sun not yet showing above the canyon walls. The road climbed steadily, the creek pounding away at the rocks, then slowing in deep pools and rushing downward again.

We stopped once and watered the horses and let them blow. I walked upstream and peered over the bank into a deep pool. I guess there were a dozen foot-long trout just idling there in the still water. When I returned to where Renfro was standing with the horses, I said, 'I don't suppose you put fish hooks and string in either sack.'

He laughed. 'You bet I did. I figured these trout would get under your hide. I've been up here fishing dozens of times. It's my favorite place when I want to get away from town and a lot of greedy people. Well, we'd better mosey. The Fanchon ranch is just around this bend.'

We mounted and rode on up the canyon. My heart quickened as I thought that finally I was about to meet this evil Fanchon family.

## CHAPTER TWENTY

Half an hour later we suddenly came out of the canyon and I found myself looking at the prettiest meadow I had ever seen in the mountains. It was big, at least a quarter of a section, with a creek meandering through the middle. Willows lined the banks with here and there a few limby cottonwoods. Surrounding the meadow was a thick growth of pine timber.

Ahead of us not more than fifty yards away was a two-story log house. On beyond were several pole corrals and slab sheds and a few other scattered outbuildings. The grass in the meadow was two or three inches tall, and I judged that by late summer it would be knee high or better and would give an excellent hay crop.

I saw several horses in the corrals, but there were only a few head of cattle in the meadow. They would not be in the high country this early, so I asked, 'Do they raise any cattle?'

Renfro shrugged. 'A shirttail full, as you can see. Nobody knows for sure how they make a living, but most folks think the boys leave long enough to hold up a stage or a bank, and then come back to hole up until they need more money. Hogan never catches them and he never gets a solid description of any outlaws that would warrant arresting the Fanchons, so it doesn't get past the gossip stage.'

'The old man?'

'Nobody knows about him, either, but I don't think he'd go off for any length of time and leave the girl here alone.'

As we approached the buildings, I saw little evidence of a woman's presence. No flowers, no white curtains at the windows, no shade trees, nothing except washing on the line back of the house. It looked to me like a workingman's ranch, and it struck me as being odd that the girl had so little influence on the lives of the men who lived here.

We were about halfway between the edge of the timber and buildings when two men came into view from behind one of the sheds. They stopped when they saw us, hands dropping to gun butts, then one of them called, 'Pa.' They came on to the gate of the nearest corral and, leaning against it, began to roll cigarettes.

We reined up about twenty feet from them, Renfro saying, 'Good morning, boys.'

Neither spoke. They looked at me, scowling, and then at Renfro, and back at me, and finally one of them spat in my direction, a derisive gesture as if saying he held me in utter contempt. They were so similar in appearance that I had the impression I was seeing double.

They were under six feet in height, but stocky. I judged they weighed about two hundred pounds. They wore beards and mustaches that so completely covered their faces that I had no idea what they looked like except for the eagle-beak noses and their eyes which were pale blue, as cold and indifferent as any eyes I had ever seen in my life.

I was so intent on studying the boys who had been called mean and evil that I was not aware of the old man's appearance until I heard him boom, 'Well, by God, if it ain't the old judge himself. Now get down off that horse. I've got a bottle in the barn yonder that'll take the hide

147

right off the back of your neck.'

'How are you, Zeke?' Renfro shook hands with Fanchon. 'No, I'd better pass up your offer this time. It's a long ride back to town and Lucinda expects me home before dark.'

I looked at the old man and had the feeling I couldn't be seeing what I thought I was seeing. He wasn't just big. He was huge. He must have stood close to seven feet and I'd say he weighed around three hundred pounds, none of it fat. His white hair hung down to his shoulders, but his face was clean shaven.

It was Fanchon's face that held my attention. It was a craggy face that looked as if it had been carved out of granite. Strong chin, an eagle-beak nose like the boys', large ears, and blue eyes that were darker than his sons' and not as cold and indifferent.

He wore a buckskin shirt and pants and beaded moccasins; his skin was swarthy, and I thought he certainly had a streak of Indian blood in him. If it hadn't been for his blue eyes, I would have said he was mostly Indian.

'I reckon you didn't come up here for the ride,' the old man said.

'No, we didn't,' Renfro said. 'This is a friend of mine, Zeke. Name's Bruce Cassidy. We rode up here to ask you a favor.'

The old man offered his hand that was as big in proportion as the rest of his body. 'Pleased to know you, Cassidy,' he said. I extended my hand and he shook it with a grip

148

that I thought would break every bone in it. 'Now what's the favor, Judge? I owe you a few.'

He stepped back, pulled a short-stemmed pipe out of his pocket and began to chew on the stem. Renfro glanced at the boys as if expecting trouble from them, but they were smoking, their pale eyes on me.

'Cassidy here is going to be a witness against some big cowmen who invaded Mule Deer County with the notion of hanging a few of us.' Renfro paused, his gaze returning to the boys again, then swung back to the old man. 'Trouble is they've tried to kill him once and they'll try again if they know where he is. I'd like for you to let him live in your cabin and keep an eye open for any dry gulchers who show up. You can bill the county for whatever rent you think you ought to get out of your cabin.'

One of the boys said, 'No.'

The other one said, 'We don't want this bastard living here.'

'Shut up, both of you,' the old man barked. 'Keep a civil tongue in your head or keep your mouth shut.' He brought his gaze to me. 'Don't pay no attention to 'em. They think they run this outfit, so I have to show 'em once in a while that they don't. I'm seventy years old, but I can still clean their plows for 'em when I have to.'

He looked me over closely, then he went on,

'Judge, it'll put us out some to look after him, but the cabin's vacant right now and I reckon nobody's gonna want to live in it for a while. You figure to cook your own meals, Cassidy?'

I nodded. 'I'd like to do some fishing and maybe some hunting to keep from eating bacon and ham all the time.'

'Sure, sure.' He nodded. 'We butcher a beef now and then mostly when Arrowhead drives their cattle up here for summer range. When we do, we'll fetch you a few steaks.'

'I'd appreciate it,' I said.

'Just stay away from down here,' the old man said, 'and don't pay no attention to anything you see. How long will he be here, Judge?'

'I hope it'll be about a month,' Renfro said. 'We expect to bring these men to trial as soon as possible, but they've got money to hire the best lawyers in the state, so they may be able to put the trial off.'

'All right.' The old man waved upstream. 'Take him on up there. Cassidy, you'll find an ax and a crosscut saw. Rustle your own wood. You can find plenty of snags and windfalls. There's blankets and dishes. If you've got grub you won't need to bother us for nothing.'

'He's gonna be here too damned long,' one of the boys muttered.

'He'd better not see anything that goes on,' the other one said in a threatening tone.

I figured that was the right time to lay into

those boys. I'd seen enough of their kind to know that if they get you on the run, they'll beat you into the ground, but if you get the bulge on them, there's a good chance they'll let you alone.

I reined my horse toward them and leaned forward in the saddle, my right hand close to the butt of my gun. I said in the meanest voice I could lay my tongue to, 'What's the matter with you bastards? I heard in town you were mean, but I don't think you are. It looks to me that you're rude like a couple of brats who were raised without learning any proper manners.'

They were amazed and shocked, I guess. For an instant they stared at me, their mouths springing open, then they went for their guns. They had them about half out of the leather when I fired a shot into the ground, the slug kicking up dirt between their feet. They froze, suddenly scared, their guns about half raised.

'Go ahead,' I said. 'You look mighty funny holding your guns kind of uncertain that way. I think you're going to get tired of holding them.'

They looked downright sheepish as they shoved their guns back into leather. The old man guffawed and slapped his legs. 'Mister, you handle your gun mighty good. I guess that'll teach you young squirts not to draw on a man when you don't know how fast he is. You're lucky to be alive.'

Looking down at the old man, I wasn't sure he was showing how he felt. I had a hunch that he pretended to be friendly and affable while the boys put on the surly act, but that behind that curtain of geniality was a core of meanness and brutality that matched that of his sons.

As for the boys, I had never seen two madder men in my life or any who had been more completely humiliated. Without a word they wheeled away from me and disappeared into the nearest shed.

'Zeke,' Renfro said in a hard voice, 'I'm not going to take it kindly if you let your boys murder Cassidy. He's important to us. We'll never convict these men without him. Now if you can't guarantee his safety, we'll go somewhere else.'

'No, no,' the old man said easily. 'They'll let him alone now. They needed to be taught a lesson and your friend done the job. Cassidy, you stay up there in your cabin and my boys'll stay down here. If we spot a stranger hunting for you, we'll get word to you.'

I could tell that Renfro was sore about the whole business and was probably having more second guesses about bringing me here, but he didn't say anything about pulling out. He jerked his head at me. 'Let's get along, Cassidy. I'll help you move in.'

We rode past the sheds. I looked back once, but I didn't see either one of the Fanchon twins. Renfro said, 'I think you did a foolish thing just then, Cassidy. The boys were just hoorawing you. Now they're going to hate you after you humiliated them the way you did.'

'Maybe,' I said, 'but I think it's more likely they're scared enough to let me alone. If I hadn't done it, they'd have run over me.'

Renfro didn't say anything, but I knew he didn't agree. To be truthful, I wasn't as sure of the Fanchon boys as I let on.

# CHAPTER TWENTY-ONE

The cabin was half a mile or more from the main buildings and near the upper end of the meadow. The creek wasn't more than fifty feet from the front door. It was running high from the spring runoff, and I could hear it from the cabin as soon as I reined up and dismounted.

I went in first and looked around. I was surprised at how clean it was. The truth was I had expected a boor's nest, but the bed was made, the floor was swept, and the dishes were all put away in a cupboard near the stove. There was even enough wood in the box behind the stove to cook one meal.

The furniture was meager, but there was all I needed: a bunk, a table, two rawhide-bottom chairs, and the stove. The door was solid, the cracks between the logs tightly chinked. Even in bad weather the cabin would be tight and warm with a fire in the cook stove. There was just one window on the door side of the cabin that looked out on the creek.

Renfro had come in behind me. He said as he looked around, 'I guess it'll do.'

'Sure,' I said. 'I'll make out fine.'

We carried the supplies into the cabin. I offsaddled and staked out my horse, then Renfro helped me put the grub away. I said, 'Better stay for dinner. You might as well help eat your own grub.'

He shook his head. 'No, I'll be getting along.' He paced the length of the cabin and back, and finally sat down. He pulled a cigar from his pocket and bit off the end, then struck a match and held the flame to the tip of the cigar. Something was eating on him, but I figured he didn't know quite how to say it, so I remained silent and let him decide what to say.

He pulled on his cigar for a moment, then he blurted, 'Damn it, Cassidy, I'll never forgive myself if you get killed up here. For God's sake, let those Fanchon boys alone.'

'I ain't figuring on bothering them,' I said. 'I'm willing to be peaceable if they are.'

He took the cigar out of his mouth and stared at it, then he said glumly, 'I thought I had figured everything out and this would be the safest place we could leave you. All I was thinking of was the invaders and the fact that they'd never think of looking for you up here, but I hadn't given enough consideration to the Fanchon boys. You see, I hadn't been up here for more than a year and they've changed. They've gotten meaner and tougher.' He stood up and almost barked at me, 'How'd you like to come back to Jackson with me?'

'Hell no,' I said. 'I'm surprised at you, Judge. You never struck me before as a nervous Nelly.'

'I'm not,' he snapped, 'but I don't like the feel of things around here. I guess I'd sleep better if you were back in my house. I hate to admit it, but Lucinda was right.'

'Don't tell her and she'll never know,' I said. 'Quit worrying, Judge. I'll be all right. In fact, I'm kind of looking forward to living up here by myself.'

He threw up his hands. 'All right, it's your choice. If anything happens to you, it'll be your own fault. You don't have to stay here.'

'That's right,' I said. 'It'll be my own fault.'

He grinned sourly. 'It didn't really make me feel any better to say that. I'll be back in two, three weeks with more grub. I guess you've got enough to run that long.'

'Sure, I've got plenty,' I said.

He left the cabin, mounted, lifted a hand to me in farewell and rode down the creek. I stood watching him until he was past the buildings and lost in the timber below them. I wasn't worried about my situation and I was a little puzzled about why Renfro was.

I built a fire and cooked dinner. After I ate, I found the ax and crosscut saw that the old man had mentioned and walked upstream into the timber. I soon found a windfall that would furnish dry wood, so I trimmed it and sawed it into three lengths so none would be too heavy for my horse to drag back to the cabin. I returned for my horse, dragged the logs to the cabin, and spent the afternoon sawing off sixteen-inch lengths that would fit the cook stove.

It was slow, hard work. I had never been an expert with a saw, so I made harder work out of it than I should have. I told myself that by the time I left, I would be an expert. I split enough wood for supper and breakfast and carried it into the cabin. By that time I was dog tired.

I had not seen anything of the old man or the boys all day. I had a hunch they had ridden off somewhere, but I didn't know for sure. My curiosity about the girl had been growing all day. I had seen her a couple of times during the afternoon, once when she left the house to gather the washing off the line and once when she went out back to the privy, but she was too far away for me to get any idea of what she was like.

If I had been real sure that the men folks were gone, I'd have ridden back to the house and talked to the girl, but I wasn't sure and I saw no reason to look for trouble. The old man's instructions had been clear enough, so I'd be smart to obey them. Too, I was a little boogery about Renfro's reversal. He must have had some grounds for asking me if I wanted to go back to Jackson, after all his trouble to get me up here.

I cooked supper, brought a bucket of water from the creek, and put some beans to soak, then washed the dishes. For a time I sat in the doorway and listened to the creek and the breeze as it rattled the limbs of the big cottonwood just below the cabin. By the time it was dusk I was ready for bed. I hadn't worked so hard for a long time and I discovered that I was softer than I had thought.

There was no lamp in the cabin, so I wouldn't be doing any reading. It didn't make any difference because there were no books or magazines in the cabin and I hadn't thought to bring any from the Judge's library. I had found some candles, so I'd make out all right.

The last of the dusk light died soon after I blew out the candle and the room turned dark. For some reason I couldn't sleep. Maybe I was too tired. I lay on my back thinking about this business I had got myself into. I decided I hadn't been very smart. Maybe I should have gone back to town with the Judge.

I guess at night a man's imagination runs wild and maybe things seem a little scarier than they are, but I got to thinking about the screen of willows along the creek and how easy it would be for a dry gulcher to hide down there and just wait for me to come out of the cabin to smoke me down. I'd never know what hit me, and I certainly had no way of being warned if a man was hiding there.

I finally dropped off to sleep. Later . . . I don't know how much later because I didn't know whether I'd been asleep for a few minutes or a few hours . . . I woke and heard a horse's hoofs thudding in the grass, then it stopped and I heard the squeal of saddle leather as someone swung down. I pulled on my pants in a hurry, my heart picking up speed as I lifted my gun from leather. I had no idea who was out there, but I figured he was up to no good or he wouldn't have come calling at this time of night.

It was too dark for me to see anything when I peered out of the window. Then I heard a light knock. I moved to the door, my gun cocked.

'Who is it?' I asked.

A woman answered, 'Garnet Fanchon. Please let me in.'

I guess it wouldn't have taken as much as a feather to have knocked me down right then. At first I thought it was some trick, then I decided no one needed to work a trick of this kind, that if the old man or the twins had wanted to get at me for some reason, they could have done it any time in the afternoon. I lifted the bar and opened the door.

The starshine was bright enough to see that someone was standing there. I said, 'Come in.'

She stepped into the cabin, saying, 'Close the door, then light a candle.'

I obeyed. When I turned from the candle to look at her, I saw that she was holding a small gun on me. 'What the hell,' I said. 'If you'd wanted to shoot me, you could have done it in the daytime.'

'I don't want to shoot you,' she said. 'I just want to look at you. While I'm doing that, you can look me over.'

'Is the gun necessary for you to look at me?' I asked.

'You've got your gun in your hand,' she said.

I had forgotten I was holding it. I laid it on the table, then I had my look. As Renfro had said, she was a pretty little thing. She was just about five feet tall and she must have weighed less than one hundred pounds. Her hair was honey colored, her eyes dark blue, and her features were regular except for her nose which was definitely pug.

Her figure impressed me more than her beauty. She wore a man's blue work shirt and pants and cowboy boots. I had never seen more curves arranged in the right order in my life. She stood with her legs slightly apart, her eyes pinned on me with a scrutiny that was embarrassing. She was, I judged, about seventeen. Her skin was tanned, so she must have spent much of her time outside since the weather had warmed up.

'You are a very pretty girl,' I said, 'and you don't need that gun to protect yourself. I don't see why you came here if you think you do.'

The gun sagged. She swallowed, then her lips began to tremble and suddenly she started to cry. She walked to the table and laid the gun beside mine, then sat down, the tears running down her cheeks.

'Now wait a minute,' I said. 'I didn't say anything to make you start bawling.'

'I'm sorry.' She pulled a blue bandanna from her pants pocket and blew her nose and wiped her eyes. 'I didn't intend to do that. I guess you think I'm crazy. I'm not. I'm just scared.'

'What are you scared of?'

'Men,' she said. 'The kind of men who come here. I didn't get a good look at you when you rode in with Judge Renfro, but I kept thinking that you must not be like the other men I see or the Judge wouldn't have brought you. I had to trust somebody and I've been hoping it would be you. I think it is. You are different. I won't need the gun and I'm sorry I brought it.'

I sat down across the table from her, deciding that this was the most extraordinary thing I ever met up with in my life. I had a feeling the girl was strong, not the weepy kind, so she must have had good reason to come here.

'Tell me about it,' I said.

'What's your name?'

'Bruce Cassidy.'

'All right, Bruce. I will tell you what I'm doing here. You'll still think I'm crazy, but I've got to do something. Right now you're the only possibility. How long are you going to be here?'

'I don't know. I'm supposed to testify at a trial in Jackson, but I don't know the date.'

She kept looking at me in that staring, appraising way that still embarrassed me. I guess she sensed that because she said, 'I came here for help and I must decide about you in case you want to give it. I've got to go on the basis that you're a trustworthy man because I'm going to put my life in your hands. I want you to get me away from here.'

Well, I had run into some strange deals, but this one got stranger all the time. The girl wasn't crazy. I was sure of that just as I was sure she was terrified. She must be in one hell of a fix or she wouldn't even be talking about going off with a strange man.

'How do you want me to take you,' I asked, 'and where to?'

'I've got a good horse,' she said. 'We can leave during the night and ride west. I've never been over the mountains, but I know that if we swing south, we'll come to a road and it will bring us to a town. If you get me there, I'll be all right. I'm a good worker. All I want is a place where I'll be safe. I'll find a job.'

No, she wasn't crazy, but she wasn't practical, either, thinking she could ride into a strange town and get a job right away. I asked, 'Why haven't you tried it before?'

'I have,' she said quickly. 'I want you to know that you'd be risking your life if you do what I ask, but I think you're tough enough to do the job. I saw you shoot at the boys this morning and you're still alive.'

'Who's keeping you here?' I asked.

'Pa,' she answered. 'I'm a good housekeeper and it's a big job taking care of the men who stay here. Pa would never find another woman who would work as hard as I do even if he paid her, which they don't do me. He'd track me and beat me half to death if I tried it alone, and if you take me, they'll track you and try to kill you.'

'That's a pleasant prospect,' I said. 'I guess I still don't know why you're scared. Is it the hard work you want to get out of?'

'No, no,' she cried. 'I'm scared because Pa says I'm old enough to go to bed with some of the men who come here, and I'm scared because I'm afraid of what he'll do to me if I refuse.'

She rose and took off her shirt. She didn't wear anything underneath. At first all I could see were her two taut, trim breasts. I expect my eyes popped out and my mouth sprung open. I don't pretend to be an expert on women's breasts, but I'd seen a few and none that came

162

close to being as perfect as these. She wasn't embarrassed in the least. She turned around to show me her back.

'I want you to see what Pa did to me the last time I tried to run away,' she said. 'That's why I won't try it by myself again.'

I stared, my breath coming out of me in a long, audible sigh of disbelief. Crosswise across her back were three long slashes that must have been made by a quirt. They were scabbed over, but it wouldn't take much to open them up again.

'I'll take you,' I said.

She slipped her shirt back on and buttoned it, then picked up the gun. She said, 'Don't make up your mind in a hurry. You've got too much to lose. I'll be back tomorrow night.'

She walked out of the cabin, closing the door behind her. A moment later I heard her horse as she rode away.

## CHAPTER TWENTY-TWO

I spent the next day fishing, cutting wood and cooking meals. In a way I did, as I had told Renfro I would, enjoy being alone, but now something else had entered into the picture that disturbed me. That something was Garnet Fanchon.

She was in my thoughts all day. She had

impressed me more than any other woman I had ever met. I say woman because, even though she was young, she had been forced to become a woman by the demands her father had made on her. I felt she was a woman in fact, if not in years.

There was much I wanted to know about her, many questions I planned to ask, but I didn't for a minute intend to go back on my promise to her. I would get her out of here, but time was the problem. I felt I had to stay until the trial was over in Jackson and that might be too late.

I turned this problem over in my mind all day. If the old man pressed her too hard, I could take her to Jackson. I was sure that Renfro would find a place for her to stay, but all hell would probably break loose. Besides, I didn't know the legal aspects of the situation. Renfro, of course, could tell me.

As far as shooting it out with the Fanchons was concerned, well I wasn't really worried about it. I suppose they were tough enough, but I'd met up with some tough men and I didn't see anything in the Fanchons that made them ten feet tall.

What Garnet had said about the old man saying she was old enough to go to bed with the men who stopped there was the part that got to me the worst. I simply could not savvy any father taking that attitude. Maybe there was nothing about the boys that was honorable, but Renfro apparently felt the old man was a little higher caliber. He wasn't, if what Garnet had said was true. Whipping her was bad enough. Making a whore out of her was a hell of a lot worse.

I had trout for supper. The creek was too high for good fishing, but I brought in three that were a foot long, so I couldn't complain. After I finished washing the dishes, I sat in the doorway and watched the day die, and all the time I felt that each minute dragged and I wondered if she would ever get here.

She did shortly after it was dark. The blackness was almost absolute. Dark clouds had moved down from the peaks and had blotted out the stars, and thunder rumbled up there somewhere to the west. I heard her horse long before she got there, and when she pulled up and stepped down, I could make out only the bare outline of her body as she moved toward the cabin.

I called, 'Hello,' wanting her to know where I was.

'Hello,' she said, and then she was there beside me, her hand resting briefly on my shoulder. 'It's a warm evening. I'll sit out here with you.'

'Good,' I said. 'You're earlier than you were last night.'

'They're all gone,' she said. 'Last night I wanted to be sure they were asleep before I left the house.'

'Suppose they get back before you do?' I asked.

She sat down beside me, her back against the log wall of the cabin. She said, 'I often ride at night. They're used to it. I don't have time during the day to ride. Pa thinks I need to keep busy doing housework and he can get pretty mean when he thinks I'm not doing all the work I should. They don't object to my riding at night, so they won't think anything of it if they find me gone. It probably wouldn't have made any difference last night, but they know you're here and I was afraid they might follow me.'

'I've got some questions,' I said.

'Go ahead,' she said. 'I'll answer them. If you're going to risk your life getting me out of here, you've got a right to ask questions.'

'Who are these men who stay here?'

'Outlaws,' she said bitterly. 'The worst kind of men you can imagine. This is an outlaw hideout. That's how pa makes his living. You've probably guessed he doesn't do it from cattle. Men have come here as long as I can remember and no questions are asked about where they're from or what they've done.

'Pa keeps a lot of supplies on hand and several extra horses. He swaps horses if theirs are worn out, getting some cash to boot. He sells them supplies. If a posse isn't too close, they usually lay over a few days.

'My job is to cook for them and keep beds

166

ready. Several times we've had men who had been wounded or were sick or just so worn out from running that they had to rest. We always let them stay here in this cabin. The others we keep in the house.'

I thought about that for a time. What she had just said explained some things and I wondered if Renfro and Hogan knew about the Fanchon place being an outlaw hideout. I decided they probably did, but it was like the rumor about the Fanchon boys robbing banks. Hogan couldn't prove it, so he hadn't bothered to raid the place. Too, there was an attitude in Mule Deer County which seemed to say that if outlaws were robbing trains and banks and big cowmen it was all right, particularly if it was somewhere else.

That might have been the real reason Hogan didn't interfere. Maybe he shared in Fanchon's profits, too. I had no way of knowing how honest a man Hogan was. In any case, it probably was mostly a proposition that if the Fanchons and the outlaws who hid out here didn't bother anyone in Mule Deer County, then Mule Deer County wouldn't bother them.

'How old are you?' I asked after a time.

'Seventeen.'

'When is your birthday?'

'August first. Why?'

That was two months away. I suppose the old man had a legal right to tell Garnet what to do until she was eighteen, so I wouldn't be getting her out of trouble if I took her to Jackson before the next two months were up. I probably would make it worse.

'Just curious,' I said finally, not wanting to tell her what I was thinking about. 'How long have you got before your pa insists on your bedding down with these men?'

'Until my birthday,' she answered. 'He says I'm a woman when I'm eighteen and it'll be time to live like one.'

'I don't savvy this,' I said. 'I just don't savvy it at all. How could any father do this?'

'He's not really my father,' she said. 'I'm adopted. Not legally, so if pa died, I'd inherit nothing from his estate. But he's raised me since I was seven years old. My parents were driving across southern Montana in a covered wagon when a renegade band of Indians attacked us and killed all the grownups. They took me with them. Pa was in the posse that chased them and killed most of them. They found me and he took me and brought me here. His wife was alive then and he knew she wouldn't be able to have any more children after she'd had the twins. His wife died two years later. I've kept house for them ever since.'

'Since you were nine years old?' I asked incredulously.

'That's right,' she said bitterly. 'They started working me when I first got here and I was only seven. Mrs. Fanchon was poorly, so she needed someone to help. I guess he worked her to death.'

This explained a lot more things. The old man may have had making a whore out of Garnet in his mind all the time. Why he hadn't brought some professionals up from Jackson I didn't know. He certainly had never accepted Garnet as a daughter. To turn his place into a hog ranch would, of course, attract more customers. Still, it seemed unbelievable that he would force this kind of a life on a girl he had raised since she was seven years old.

'It's been hell, hasn't it?' I asked.

'Yes it has,' she said in the same bitter tone she had used before. 'I would feel no regrets if I left tonight and never saw any of the Fanchons again. I've had to fight the boys to keep them out of my bed for the last five years. I stabbed one of them with a knife about six months ago and I promised I'd kill one of them if they tried it again, so they haven't. I think they're more afraid of pa than they are of me. I told them I'd tell him if they tried it again. I will say that for him. They would have abused me a lot more if it hadn't been for him.'

It struck me that if she wasn't the old man's daughter and hadn't been legally adopted, he had no right to make her stay here. I said, 'I had been thinking about taking you to Jackson if it gets unbearable. The Judge would find you a place to live and help you get a job. I'm obligated to stay here until after I testify at the trial. I don't know when that will be. The Judge talks about a month, but things like that get dragged out, so it might be longer.'

She reached out and took my hand. She said, 'Don't take me to Jackson. Please! The only way is to go over the mountains and keep on going.'

'Why?' I asked. 'If the Judge . . .'

'He can't help me,' she said. 'Pa gets whatever he wants down there, so I'd wind up coming back. I can't face that. You don't know what he'd do to me.'

I didn't push it that night, but when the Judge came with my supplies two weeks later, I told him the whole story. He gave me a strange look. He didn't have to say it. I knew dammed well that Garnet was dead right, so it seemed plain enough that the officials in Jackson knew what the Fanchons had been doing and simply looked the other way.

'Stay out of it, Cassidy,' he said. 'I don't think I can help her if you bring her to town.'

'You said you didn't know much about Garnet,' I said accusingly, 'but you've known all the time.'

'No I haven't,' he said sharply. 'I don't think that Hogan or anyone else in Jackson knows. It's just that there's a sort of working agreement with the Fanchons. If we keep it, they don't bother us or anything that belongs to us. We've had our hands full fighting the cowmen without taking on an outlaw family that doesn't bother us. The old man has been honest with me and he's helped me a few times, like giving you a place to stay. I just don't want to buck him. Besides, the girl might be lying about what he intends to do.'

'I saw what her back looked like,' I said hotly. 'That was no lie.'

'He might have beaten her about something else,' he said.

I stood there looking at him in the bright June sunshine. He looked a lot smaller to me than he ever had before. He just didn't seem to be the upstanding representative of justice and courage that I had thought he was.

'Judge,' I said. 'I'll still play along if there's time, but if the trial isn't held before August first, I'll be gone.'

'Don't do it, Cassidy,' he said. 'I know the old man. He's a vindictive bastard. He'll kill you.'

I didn't think until after he left to ask if they were making any headway in setting a trial date, but he would have told me if they had. All I could think of was that Judge Renfro had been a man I respected. I didn't respect him now.

# CHAPTER TWENTY-THREE

The weeks I spent in the Fanchon cabin were the most enjoyable of my life. In many ways it was an extended vacation with nothing to do except take care of my physical needs: I fished, I hunted, I cut wood, and when there was nothing else to do, I just sat in my doorway looking at the willows and cottonwoods along the creek, or the dark edge of timber on the far side of the meadow, and enjoyed being lazy.

Mostly it was Garnet who made those weeks so good. Sometimes she came just after dark, sometimes at midnight or one o'clock in the morning. If the old man or the twins caught on to where she was going, they said nothing to her, or at least she did not mention it to me.

She was everything I had ever wanted in a girl and I made up my mind before the first month was up that I'd take her with me all the way to Delaney, Oregon. I didn't know what Marge would say. I didn't even know for sure if she meant it when she'd talked about making me a partner, but I aimed to find out.

I didn't say anything about this to Garnet at the time, though I did tell her about the K Bar and Marge, and said I had a job there whenever I wanted to go back. Sometimes we just sat and talked. She told me about the outlaws who had spent time here, and as much as she could remember about her childhood and her parents and that fatal trip across southern Montana and her brief captivity with the Indians.

I told her about my life, assuring her once that when I got away from there, my gunfighting days were over. I had paid my debt when I'd shot and killed Hank Gibson, and this trip to Wyoming had opened my eyes about the problems between the big cowmen and the settlers. Not that my sympathies had changed. It was simply a matter of realizing that it was not a black-white situation as I had thought it was. I had come here to help the people of Mule Deer County and I would do what I could, but I admitted to myself that I would be glad when it was over and I was on my way back to Oregon.

I'd make a pot of coffee when Garnet got to the cabin and sometimes she'd bring a couple pieces of cake or part of a pie she had made that day and we'd sit by the fire and talk, or sometimes sit and say nothing. To me this was a remarkable thing, that we enjoyed each other's company enough to just sit in silence. I knew she had no chance to catch up on her sleep during the day, and I told her she had better stay in the house and get a good night's sleep.

She looked at me a long time, then she said softly, 'Bruce, this is the first time since my folks were killed that I have been happy. Would you take any of it away from me?'

'No, but . . .'

'No buts,' she said firmly. 'There'll be plenty of time for me to sleep after you get me away from here and you're on your way to Oregon.'

What could I say to that? Nothing, so I kissed her. It was the first time. I simply opened my arms and she came to me. I hugged her and kissed her hard, and suddenly she began to cry. Finally she turned away from me and wiped her eyes.

'Isn't that silly?' she said. 'I've wanted you to do that ever since I came here that first night. Now that you have, I start to bawl. I guess it's just because I feel so good.'

It seemed damned silly to me, all right, and I never could see any logic in a woman bawling because she was having a good time. I didn't know much about women, that part of my life having been neglected, but I had enough common sense to know that it was time to keep my mouth shut.

A thought did strike me that she was pretending, simply using me to get her out of here, but the thought didn't linger. I didn't believe she could turn on her tears the way she did if she was not being honest with me.

I decided there was no sense in putting off telling her what I was thinking, so I said, 'I want to take you with me to Oregon. We can get married on the other side of the Big Horns or when we get to Oregon. We'll see what Marge Delaney thinks of it. Maybe she'd like for you to take over the house. She'd rather work outside than do housework. I don't have much money, but I've always had work . . .'

'Bruce, stop it,' she said sharply. 'Of course you'll always have work. So will I. Maybe we'll never be rich, but we won't starve.'

I liked that. She was young and strong and so was I. I'd seen too many women who bitched about how hard they had to work and how tough their lives had been. I guess it was true of most homesteaders' wives, but I always figured it didn't have to be that way, that it was part of a decision they had made. I had to change that a little after I thought about it because it usually was the man who made the decision, and the woman had no choice but to go along.

Anyhow, I never had sensed any of the feeling-sorry-for-herself attitude in Garnet, and it looked to me as if she had plenty of reason to have it if she had let herself. After she left that night, I lay in bed and dreamed my dreams and thought about Garnet and Marge Delaney, and how it would be when we got to Oregon.

Judge Renfro returned early in July with more supplies. The instant I saw his face, I knew something was wrong. I didn't ask him what had happened, figuring that he'd tell me in his good time. We carried the grub into the

175

cabin, then he sat down and I poured him a cup of coffee.

He looked sick. More than that, it struck me that suddenly he had become old and fragile. He said, 'Cassidy, maybe we've both been wasting our time. They've moved the invaders from the fort to Cheyenne, lock, stock, and barrel. I did everything in the court I could to stop it, but they've got the power on their side.'

'That's loco,' I said. 'Why?'

'They claim the bastards wouldn't get a fair trial in Mule Deer County and they might be right, folks feeling the way they do, but they won't get a fair trial in Cheyenne, either, looking at it from our point of view. They'll just get turned loose.'

'It suits me,' I said. 'I'll be leaving tomorrow. I've lost my taste for this deal anyhow.'

'No, no,' he said quickly. 'You can't do that. Not yet. I'm doing all I can to hurry the trial up. At least we'll use the trial to put witnesses on the stand to show what they did and what they planned to do. We've got to get it over with or Mule Deer County will go broke feeding those sons of bitches. I'll be back in a few days to get you, maybe a week.'

'All right,' I said. 'I'll wait a week.'

I told Garnet about it that night. She smiled and said, 'We'll go in a week then. He won't get that trial started so soon. That's their game. They'll keep postponing the trial and in the end they'll just call it off and turn the invaders loose.'

'No, they won't do that,' I said.

'You'll see,' she said.

I didn't argue, but it seemed unreasonable to think that the men who had murdered Red Dawson and Peewee Curry would be turned loose without the formality of a trial to acquit them. So I said, 'If they do get the trial started within a week, I'll testify and then come back and get you. If they don't, we'll leave at the end of the week.'

'It's time,' she said. 'For weeks I've thought of just two things, Bruce, you and getting away from here.'

I felt that way, too, but in a way I hated to leave. It was a fine way to live, with everything I wanted and no responsibility. But I guess nothing in life is permanent and it was up to me to get Garnet to Oregon and make our life there as good as it was here.

Renfro returned in a week. I was sawing wood when I saw him ride past the house. I dropped the crosscut and walked around to the front of the cabin. He wasn't leading a pack horse, but that probably didn't mean anything since I had told him I'd wait only a week and he knew I had enough grub to last that long. Still, I was uneasy as I watched him ride up. When he came close enough for me to see his face, I knew I had reason to be uneasy.

When Renfro had been here the last time, I

177

had felt he had become old and fragile. Now, staring at him, I had a feeling he was ready to die. He dismounted, then stood for a moment beside the horse, one hand gripping the horn. I stood looking at him, and it struck me that he was not only ready to die but that he was to all intents and purposes a living dead man, that he had lost his purpose in life.

He stared at me, his eyes bloodshot. He said, 'It's like I mentioned last time I saw you, Cassidy. We wasted our time.'

I thought of what Garnet had said about turning the invaders loose, but I still didn't believe it. I said, 'Come on in, Judge, and have a cup of coffee. I'll fry some meat if you can stay.'

'No, I can't stay,' he said, 'and I can't eat. I haven't eaten anything solid for three days, but I will take that cup of coffee.'

He walked into the cabin and sat down at the table. I got him a cup and poured the coffee. He stared at it a moment, then lifted the cup to his lips and took a drink, and set it back on the table.

'It seems like a nightmare, Cassidy,' he said. 'You know how it's been with me. I moved to Jackson before it was really a town and before there was any law in Mule Deer County. I devoted my life since then to the principle that I could bring law to a lawless country and avoid vigilante action and that kind of thing you see so often in a new country. To a great extent I succeeded. It was a very satisfying experience. But now?'

He took another sip of coffee and set the cup down. 'Well, we can do things right in our back yard, but by God, the state is another yard. We can't touch it. I've been in Cheyenne ever since I saw you except for travel time. I talked to everybody I could from the governor on down. I couldn't do a thing. Mule Deer County is broke. Of course no other county or the state will foot the bill for trying those murdering bastards, so they're turned loose.'

Garnet had been right and I'd been so sure it couldn't happen. I said, 'I guess I know how you feel. There's no justice in turning murderers loose like that.'

'Of course not,' Renfro said, 'and it's hard to accept when you know the law can be used to bring about justice. There is one other thing you'd better know. They still consider you a threat because it's possible that someday we might bring legal action against the ones we can get at like Chauncey Dunn and Slim Yancey. They don't know where you are as far as I know, but they are guessing we've got you hidden out somewhere and they've put a price on your head. In other words, you are to be silenced.'

'I guess the Fanchons would sell me out if they knew that,' I said.

'They'll hear it sooner or later, so you'd better be sloping out of here.' He rose, took a

179

small buckskin bag from his pocket and handed it to me. 'I promised you that you'd be paid for your time. This is the best I could do. I wish it was more, but then I wish it hadn't turned out this way.'

I took the bag and shook hands with him. He walked back to his horse, mounted, and rode away without even looking back. I went inside and counted the coins in the bag. One hundred dollars in gold! Well, it was not bad pay for the time I had spent in Mule Deer County, but, like Renfro, I wished the whole business had not turned out this way.

I cooked and ate dinner, and then the afternoon hung heavily on my hands. I was ready to go, and if it hadn't been for Garnet, I'd have been on my way as soon as I'd eaten. I didn't think there was any immediate danger, but I was uneasy and I had no intention of staying here any longer than necessary. If there was a price on my head as Renfro had told me, there would soon be plenty of men trying to collect it as long as I stayed in the country.

My things were packed and ready to tie behind my saddle by the middle of the afternoon. I figured Garnet had seen the Judge ride in and leave by himself, and she'd be ready to go as soon as she could get away. That might be midnight because I knew the old man and the twins were at home, but she didn't wait. I was surprised to see her leave the house late in the afternoon and head straight for my cabin.

I waited in front of the cabin, knowing that something was up or she wouldn't be here at this time of day. She reined to a stop, a cloud of dust lifting all around her. She cried out, 'Saddle up, Bruce. We've got to get out of here. Now!'

## CHAPTER TWENTY-FOUR

I don't know what I expected her to say, but it wasn't that. I stood there, staring at her, and she said impatiently, 'Go on. Saddle up.'

'What happened?' I asked.

She opened her mouth to say something, then closed it. I had no intention of moving until she told me what was going on, and I guess she read it in my face.

'The twins just got back from town,' she said. 'They heard that the big cowmen have offered five hundred dollars to anyone who kills you. They were pretty worked up about it and were coming right up here after you, but Pa cooled them off and said it might be only a rumor that somebody had started after the invaders were turned loose. He said there wasn't any sense in taking a chance on getting hurt if it wasn't so.

'The Judge had told Pa about what had

happened in Cheyenne. He said for the twins to ride over to the Arrowhead cow camp and talk to Slim Yancey. They're over there now. It's just on the other side of that ridge yonder. If Yancey says they really will pay the five hundred dollars, the boys and Pa will come back and shoot you.'

That was good enough for me. I got my bedroll and rifle from the cabin and saddled my horse. I stepped up, glancing back at the Fanchon house. I wasn't quite satisfied with Garnet's story. It wouldn't take all three of them to talk to Slim Yancey and give me a chance to ride out. Since Renfro had told the old man what had happened, he knew I wouldn't be staying here.

I didn't see any movement around the house or the corrals. Garnet was sitting her saddle, impatience growing in her. She demanded, 'Aren't you ready to ride yet?'

'Yeah, I'm ready,' I said.

We turned upstream toward the fringe of timber that marked the west end of the meadow. On beyond were the jagged snow peaks that marked the divide. Somewhere among those mountains was a road that went over a pass. It might not be easy to find, but we had to find it. We had no choice. We couldn't ride downstream to Jackson and I couldn't stay here. The only logical thing was to get out of the country the fastest and quickest way we could, and that way was to go over the Big

Horns.

We were within twenty feet of the first pine when the old man stepped out of a willow thicket along the creek, his rifle held on the ready. I had expected something like this because it just wasn't logical that all three Fanchons would ride off and leave their five hundred dollar prize free to ride away, but I hadn't expected it so soon. I was caught, and all I could do was to pull up and sit my saddle and give myself a mental cussing.

'You ain't going nowhere, mister,' the old man said in a harsh tone. 'Turn around and head back to the cabin. You make a quick move of any kind and you're a dead man.'

'Pa, you can't do this,' Garnet screamed. 'You've got no cause to kill him. He's never hurt you.'

He turned his gaze to Garnet, the rifle still held on me. He said, 'Five hundred dollars is plenty of reason,' he said. 'Dragging you off with him is another good reason. You figger he'll take care of you, don't you? Fix you up in a fine house and all? Well, by God, you're in for a surprise. You're staying right here and working out what you owe me for raising you and you'll keep on working for me till you're twenty-one.'

'And then what will I do?' she cried.

He shrugged his massive shoulders. 'It makes me no never mind what you do, but I reckon you can find a whorehouse in Sheridan

183

or Billings or Miles City where you can work. You'll be purty well worn out by then.'

'I sure will,' she said bitterly.

I sat there thinking about how I'd walked into the old man who'd been waiting for me. I knew that whatever I did I had to do now. Once the old man had my guns, I was a goner. My horse had fidgeted around with a little encouragement from me so now he was turned broadside to the old man. I had to do this right, for Garnet's sake as well as my own.

The old man was making no pretense of being friendly as he had the day I had arrived with the Judge. He was just plain ugly, and I was dead sure he'd shoot me out of my saddle on the slightest provocation.

His eyes were still on Garnet. 'You thought you were purty damned cute, didn't you? We figgered you wasn't hurting nothing, so we let you do it. When the Judge told me about the invaders, I knew you'd be making your play this afternoon. Well, you bet on a slow horse, girl. When we get back to the house, I'll beat hell out of you. I reckon you'll never try it again. Now head back, both of you. I'm tired of talking.'

'I've got to tighten my cinch,' I said.

I dismounted before he had a chance to tell me to stay on the horse. I guess he was a little surprised. Anyhow, he lost a few seconds while he thought about it. If he'd been a little smarter, or if he'd had time to consider it, he'd

184

have known I was bulling him because it wasn't likely I'd have needed to tighten my cinch this soon after I'd started out. If he had seen through what I was doing, he'd have shot me out of the saddle the first move I made.

Anyhow, those few seconds meant life for me. I was on the ground and my gun was in my hand when I stepped into view in front of my horse. He had figured out what I was up to by that time and he fired, but he was a split second too slow. His bullet made a hole in my shirt under my left arm and raised a gash along my ribs.

He didn't fire again because my bullet caught him squarely in the chest and slammed him back a step, his rifle dropping from his hands. I think he must have been dead before he went down, falling slowly and ponderously like a great pine. I ran to him and threw his rifle toward the creek. I had no need to feel for his pulse. His face had already taken on the blankness of death.

I holstered my gun and wheeled back to my horse. Garnet was staring at me, wide-eyed. She whispered, 'I didn't think you could do it, Bruce. I didn't see how you could. I thought I'd been the cause of your death.'

I stepped into the saddle, asking, 'How do you figure that out?'

'Because you would have been gone hours ago if it hadn't been for me,' she said as we rode west.

'I figured you were worth waiting for,' I said, the timber closing around us. 'How long will it take the twins to ride to Arrowhead cow camp?'

'An hour,' she answered.

So we had less than two hours jump on them if they started after us as soon as they got back, and I was sure they would. I had fished several miles up the creek during the weeks I had been here, so I knew the country that far, but only that far. That was where the twins had the advantage. They had lived here most of their lives and they undoubtedly had been all over the Big Horns.

For about three miles the creek followed a narrow valley. The stream ran slowly for those three miles, meandering back and forth across the floor of the valley, then the valley became a canyon and for the next mile the climb was a steep one, the creek roaring down that narrow defile as if it were in a hurry to reach Powder River. Farther up the country flattened out again and I remembered a small clearing with a fallen-down cabin that some homesteader had built years ago. That was where we would make our stand.

We rode hard for the first three miles, then had to slow up through the narrow canyon. It was hard going, switching from one bank to the other or wading the stream and returning to the bank again, working our way around boulders and windfalls and deep pools. The twins wouldn't travel any faster than we were, but I wanted all of that two hours if I could manage it.

Once when we stopped to blow our horses, Garnet asked, 'What are we going to do? Can we outrun them?'

'No,' I answered. 'Not in rough country like this that they know and we don't.'

'Well, what are we going to do?'

'We'll stop and wait for them to catch up with us,' I said. 'There's a clearing ahead of us that'll work.'

'You mean you're going to stop and wait for them to fight you?' she demanded.

'That's about the size of it,' I said.

'I can help,' she cried. 'I can use a rifle if you'll let me have yours.'

'Sure you can help,' I said, 'but you're not going to. I've got an idea and we'll play it out. I don't figure on just running and give them a chance to dry gulch us. I'd rather dry gulch them.'

She nodded, trusting me. I was gratified. I knew and I'm sure she knew that she was in trouble if they caught her. She'd told me enough times about how they'd have raped her if it hadn't been for the old man. Now he was gone, and if the twins caught her, they'd rape her and kill her. I hadn't had any dealings with the Fanchon boys, but Garnet had told me enough to convince me that they were worse than anything I had heard about them.

It was still daylight when we reached the clearing. We dismounted. I told Garnet to take care of the horses and to tie them in the timber some distance from the creek. Then I started piling up all the wood I could find. Some of it was driftwood from along the creek, some were limbs I found back among the pines, but most of it was from the tumbled-down, old cabin.

I had a big fire going by the time she returned. She said, 'I didn't take much time to get a sack of grub put together. All I've got is what's left of a roast and some biscuits.'

'It'll do,' I said. 'Maybe we'll get lucky and shoot a deer tomorrow. Anyhow, I guess we'll get to the other side before we starve to death.'

'We'll have to,' she said. 'There aren't any people living in the high country. At least none that I ever heard of.'

We ate roast and biscuits as we crouched by the fire, washing the food down with water from the creek. When we finished, I said, 'I want you to stay in the timber and not come out for any reason. I don't figure on them getting me, but if they do, there's a good chance they won't find you in the darkness. Maybe they'll go back home. If that happens, take the horses and keep riding.'

She was silent for a time, looking at me in the firelight, then she said, 'There are only three things that the twins love: money and

188

women and whisky, and in that order. They'll take you back for the money, they'll hunt till they find me, and they'll drink up the five hundred dollars they get from Yancey.'

I thought about that a moment, then handed her my .45. 'I'll have to keep the rifle,' I said. 'Use this gun on yourself if there's nothing else you can do.'

She took the Colt, then looked at me. 'Bruce, I haven't made it any worse for you, have I?'

'No,' I said, wondering why she asked, then I decided to lie a little. 'If it hadn't been for you warning me, I'd have been caught back there in the cabin.'

'I'm glad,' she said. 'I love you, Bruce. I haven't known what it was to love anyone since my parents were killed, until I met you. I couldn't stand it if I thought I'd cost you your life. I thought that was going to happen when Pa stepped up.'

I took her into my arms and kissed her. I said, 'We'll make it. Just be sure you stay out of the way and don't make a sound. Now get back into the trees and stay there until it's over.'

I carried one saddle and blanket into the timber for her. I said, 'Sleep if you can, but in any case, stay back out of sight till I holler.'

Returning to the fire, I piled more wood on it, then found a short log and pulled it back so it was in the fringe of light. I covered it with a blanket, set the saddle on one end, and placed my hat on the saddle. It wasn't much of a dummy, but I didn't have anything else to work with. I had to go on the basis that the twins weren't very smart. Anyhow, it was the best I could do. In the thin firelight, it should work.

The night was black, with heavy clouds moving down from the peaks as they so often did this time of year. The fire was an island of light in a dark world. For a long time I heard nothing except the wind in the trees and the rumble of thunder to the west, and now and then the scampering of some small animal as it darted across the mat of pine needles that had been piling up since time began. Then I heard them, the faint click of metal on rocks. They were still in the canyon, I thought.

I stood up and cocked my rifle. They would be drawn to the fire, of course, and if they were stupid enough to give their position away, I'd get them. That was the best I could hope for. The sound of hoofs came closer, so I knew they were out of the canyon and approaching the clearing. Then for a time I heard nothing.

Now time seemed to stand still. They might be circling the clearing; they might be on me before I knew it. I stood with my back to a pine, trying to make no sound, yet even my breathing seemed loud enough to give me away.

Then suddenly the night silence was ripped apart by the crackling of rifle fire as they riddled the blanket and log with lead. I was tempted to fire back because I knew where they were, but I wanted a sure chance and I knew there was nothing sure about firing into the darkness.

I didn't count the shots, but there must have been a dozen. They ran into the clearing toward the fire, one of them whooping, 'I guess that'll teach the bastard to go to sleep when we're on his tail.'

I waited until they were well into the circle of firelight, then I called, 'You want me?'

They wheeled, plainly shocked by the sound of my voice. Their rifle barrels swung toward me, but neither got off a shot. I was almost as fast and accurate with a rifle at this range shooting from my hip as I was with a six-shooter. One of them was dead with a bullet in his brisket before he hit the ground. The other one fell, bounced up and yanked his .45 from leather, but my third shot finished him.

I yelled, 'All right, Garnet.'

She came running through the trees, barking her shins and falling and crying out. I yelled at her, 'Slow up. I'm all right.'

'Thank God,' she said, and then she was in my arms, holding me as if she would never let me go. 'It was the hardest thing I ever had to do, staying back there and not knowing what was happening.'

'It's over,' I said. 'We'll ride on a piece and then try to get some sleep.'

'We'll need it,' she said. 'Bruce, do you understand what this means to me? Not just our safety, but life. A new life! I feel as if I had just been let out of a trap.'

Yes, a new life, I thought. It meant going back to an old one, but it was new because I had Garnet, and I was freed from the old bitterness that had plagued me since my father's death. I would never like big cattlemen. I would go on hating them, but that hatred was not the compulsion it had been for so long. I guess it was the same with me that it was with Garnet. I, too, had been let out of a trap.

We hope you have enjoyed this Large Print book. Other Chivers Press or Thorndike Press Large Print books are available at your library or directly from the publishers.

For more information about current and forthcoming titles, please call or write, without obligation, to:

Chivers Large Print
published by BBC Audiobooks Ltd
St James House, The Square
Lower Bristol Road
Bath BA2 3SB
UK
email: bbcaudiobooks@bbc.co.uk
www.bbcaudiobooks.co.uk

OR

Thorndike Press
295 Kennedy Memorial Drive
Waterville
Maine 04901
USA
www.gale.com/thorndike
www.gale.com/wheeler

All our Large Print titles are designed for easy reading, and all our books are made to last.